WORK FOR A MILLION

WORK FOR A MILLION

by

Eve Zaremba

An Amanita Publication

For Ottie, with all my love.

First Printing September 1987
Second Printing August 1988

CANADIAN CATALOGUING IN PUBLICATION DATA

Zaremba, Eve
Work for a Million

ISBN 0-921299-00-1

PS8599.A74W67 1987   C813'.54   C87-094426-6
PR9199.3.Z37W67 1987

Cover and Book Design by Elizabeth Martin
Typesetting by Moveable Type Inc.
Amanita Logo Design by Dougal Haggart

ORDER INFORMATION

AMANITA ENTERPRISES
P.O. BOX 784 STATION P
TORONTO , ONTARIO, CANADA
M5S 2Z1

AMANITA—a genus of mushrooms which is a study in contrast. It contains the most deadly and most delicious species of fleshy fungi.

1

IT WAS EARLY EVENING. I sipped a quiet drink alone in one of Toronto's downtown bars. My bank account was in good shape, I had just gotten a new truck and was looking forward to driving it home to Vancouver. I planned to take the long southern route west, via the U.S., visiting Arizona, New Mexico, California and head north from there. Deep in my thoughts and my second drink I realized that someone was speaking to me.

"How would you like to work for a million?" No matter who you are and how much you claim to despise money, mention of a million will make your head spin. It certainly turned mine around. She was standing very still, a wine glass turning slowly between her fingers. Her eyes were blurred with drink, and a well trained grin disfigured her face. I had seen her before like this; she hung around fashionable midtown bars and chic restaurants. Her name was Shelley, she knew everyone and everyone knew her; it wasn't hard to guess how she made a living.

"You're Helen Keremos, aren't you?" she continued.

"Yes." It was true and I didn't feel like arguing with her about it.

"Well, I know a man who wants to hire you. He should be here soon. His name is Tommy Burrows."

"What does he want? And what's this about 'working for a million'?"

She played with her drink and looked at me through her false eyelashes and giggled.

"Interesting, isn't it? He will tell you... A very nice man..." She broke off, looked towards the entrance through the smoke-filled room, and continued: "There he is! Wait! He'll be right over."

She moved away, making her way carefully among the tables towards a tall, well dressed youngish man. They met, spoke briefly, Shelley nodded towards me and continued on towards the bar. The man walked up to where I sat at a corner table, stopped, gave me a wide, charming smile.

"My name is Burrows. Shelley says you are Helen Keremos, a private investigator." He waited for an answer.

"Yes."

"May I sit down and buy you a drink? I have a proposition to put to you."

"Sure." In spite of myself I was intrigued.

He sat down, waved at a passing waiter, who nodded. Burrow's preference in drinks was obviously well known in this establishment. He made himself comfortable, lit a cigarette. Close up, Burrows was older than he had seemed across the room, well past thirty. He had that smoothness of manner associated with young corporate lawyers and advertising executives. His clothes were everything a well dressed young man about town would wear this year. Yet there was an uncertainty about him, as if his instructions were unclear. Somehow he wasn't as sure of his ground as he should have been. Burrows was a lawyer in a well known Bay Street law firm, and a big shot to Shelley and the waiter, but his real function was messenger boy for his betters. As it turned out, all he was doing was inviting me to meet with his boss, a Mr. Arthur B. Sedgwick, Q.C., senior partner in the firm of Sedgwick, Sedgwick, McClelland, Potter and Bono. Mr. Sedgwick had a client who could use my services. He wished to meet me the next morning at 11:30 at his office to discuss the case. I was disappointed. What had started out promising was turning into a bore.

"I don't want a job. Unless it's interesting and well paid, naturally. Is it?" I asked Burrows.

"Yes to both, I assure you." He was earnest as hell.

"So tell me about it. Sell me."

"Now really. I can't discuss it here. Mr. Sedgwick will explain. He was very insistent that you come. He wants to meet you. I assure you it will be to your advantage." Burrows started to sweat, perhaps afraid he wouldn't manage to deliver me to his master.

"What makes you think I want to meet him, on your say so? And what's all this about 'work for a million'? Million what?"

"Ah!" He brightened at my interest. Then sobered suddenly, "Did Shelley mention anything about a million dollars? She shouldn't have. Most indiscreet. I must tell her—"

I broke in: "If you want me to see your Mr. Sedgwick you'd better tell me something that will hold my interest. So what about 'work for a million'?"

"That's just Shelley being extra cute. But it is true in a way. The client is a millionaire."

"So what? Having millions isn't contagious. What's in it for me? What do you want done?"

"Look, I really can't tell you. But I will give you $100 cash right now just to show up tomorrow and see Mr. Sedgwick. If you don't like his proposition you can just walk out. Fair enough?" He reached for his wallet and looked at me.

"Fair enough," I said. An easy hundred is an easy hundred.

2

NEXT DAY at 11:30 a.m. I was in an elevator of a downtown office building surrounded by an assortment of nine-to-five humanity. It had been a late night, dinner, drinks and good company. By rights, at this very moment I should have been recuperating over my second cup of coffee and the entertainment section of the *Globe & Mail*. Instead, I was on my way to the thirty-ninth floor of an ugly slab of glass and concrete. All for a lousy hundred bucks! The whole thing was absurd. Just when I was about to get free of Toronto after five weeks spent getting ready for the road. Five weeks spent choosing, buying, testing, and fitting my new four-wheel drive GMC. Five weeks spent by the phone at an apartment of a friend who was out of town on a film shoot; five weeks of impatience and expectation—and five weeks of parties and farewells. Here I was letting myself be bribed into meeting Mr. Arthur B. Sedgwick who was bound to be a schmuck.

By the time I reached his office I had persuaded myself that the hundred bucks had nothing to do with it. It was sheer curiosity which had brought me here. And it always makes me feel better to be paid to satisfy my curiosity. Once I had that clear I felt lots better. Better able to enjoy whatever I found in Suite 3914 of this gold-plated bank tower.

The law firm of Sedgwick, Sedgwick, McClelland, Potter and Bono did very well for itself. It occupied two floors with southern exposure towards the harbour and Toronto Island park and western windows overlooking the thicket of other downtown skyscrapers. The lobby was overdecorated, colour-coordinated to a fault and filled with pictures, plants, rugs and other high-tone office necessities. It contained a number of patient men absorbed in flipping through up-to-date copies of *Fortune, Toronto Life* and *The Ontario Law Review,* and one glamorous receptionist busy on the phone. I had visions of being kept here waiting till I put down roots in one of the enormous planters full of greenery. But I was wrong. Immediately after my name was communicated to some power within, a poised, competent-looking woman emerged, introduced herself as Mr. Sedgwick's secretary and took me to the great man's private office.

It was quite a place. Library of some English country house would come close to describing it. Entering into this splendour from the modern-office-decor and everyday hubbub of the outer office was quite an experience. It produced a slight feeling of disorientation. For one thing, there was absolutely nothing phoney about the room—except its location, of course. The furniture and fittings were not 'done' by a professional decorator, not even the books which lined the walls had been bought by the yard. Clearly, everything there had been carefully, lovingly and with much trouble collected by the man who now stood in the middle of a superb Persian carpet and welcomed me. Arthur B. Sedgwick was a small, spare man in his late fifties. His eyes were icy blue, his clothes perfect and perfectly understated. His manner was gracious without being patronizing and conveyed the aura of another time and place. Like his office. The other three men present seemed totally insignificant beside him. One of these men was Tom Burrows, smiling obsequiously as ever. He certainly was insignificant and, having fulfilled his function of delivering me as per orders, disappeared quietly never to be seen again. The other two men were introduced as Ben Bono, one of the partners in the firm and Charles Weller, whose position was unclear. After Burrows' departure, the four of us—Sedgwick, Bono, Weller and I—sat down and exchanged polite preliminaries proper to the occasion: Blue Jays' chances in the pennant race, the Toronto weather and state of its traffic, and our respective wellbeing.

Sedgwick cleared his throat and said, "Miss Keremos, we are concerned with the possibility of availing ourselves of your professional services in a somewhat sensitive and difficult matter. I need hardly say that it is also highly confidential. Before we proceed, have I your assurance that none of what we discuss here will go any further, whether you accept this assignment or not?"

"That depends on what you're about to tell me. I cannot promise anything in advance, not even silence. However, a private investigator's prime stock in trade is keeping her mouth shut. If I didn't do that I would be out of business in a month."

Sedgwick smiled approvingly.

"Yes, of course. However, would it help if I assured you that we are not asking you to get involved in anything illegal?"

"It would help some but not enough. It's not what's on the law books that makes the difference to me but what sort of a game is being played. For instance you could be out to shaft someone, all perfectly legally. Depending on circumstances I might feel obliged to warn that someone. What I am saying is that not everything goes as far as I am concerned. So, no, Mr. Sedgwick you will just have to trust me with your secret, whatever it is. If I feel OK about it I will keep mum whether I take the job or not. But no promises in advance. Besides, if I am not trustworthy, what good is my word anyway?"

"True, very true. I accept that." Sedgwick turned to the other two men. "Well, gentlemen, are you also satisfied that we can proceed?" Bono just nodded. Weller spoke up and I listened with interest hoping to get a clue to his part in this charade.

"Sure, Arthur, if you think it's all right. You set up this meeting, you're Sonia's legal counsel. We'll go along with your decision." Was Weller the millionaire client? It didn't seem likely. And who the hell was Sonia?

Sedgwick replied, "Thank you, Chuck. Yes, I think we can tell Miss Keremos our problem and make her a definite proposition if she is interested. I am satisfied." So all that palaver about 'confidentiality' was so much hot air. Sedgwick was merely going through the motions, presumably to test me. Perhaps to see whether I had any ethics? or any sense? or how hungry I was for the job? Whatever the test, I seemed to have passed it. Sedgwick spoke again, this time to Ben Bono. "Ben, go ahead. Tell Miss Keremos the whole story."

3

BENJAMIN BONO WAS ONE of the new breed of 'ethnic' lawyers coming out of Canada's law schools in ever increasing numbers. As I found out later, he was second generation Italian, youngest of three children of an immigrant couple from Ancona. Of the other two, the older boy was now an electrical contractor and the daughter was a teacher. His father had been a construction worker who had lost a hand building Toronto's subway system. Compensation for that, Mother Bono's years on the job in a soap factory plus lots of after school work had helped put the three children through college. All that was not too surprising. Assimilation and upward mobility are not unheard of. However, for the likes of Ben Bono to become partner in an old Anglo establishment firm such as Sedgwick, Sedgwick, McClelland and Potter was something else again. Ben Bono had to have something pretty special going for him. I wondered what that might be.

"Miss Keremos, I am sure you've heard of the IntraProvincial Lottery? Yes?" I nodded. Who in Canada hadn't? "And perhaps you've also heard of Miss Sonia Deerfield?" I shook my head. "No."

"Ah. Sonia Deerfield is a fine singer and show business personality. On her way to stardom, as we here are all convinced." The other two men nodded their heads in unison. "At a recent draw of the IntraProvincial Sonia won a million dollars." Bono paused briefly while all four of us paid silent homage to the six zeros. He continued, "Since then she has been harassed, importuned and even threatened. That's where you come in. We want you to protect her and put a stop to this harassment." So now I knew a thing or two about Ben Bono. One, he came to the point quickly and two, he cared what happened to Sonia Deerfield. I had expected Sedgwick to jump in right about here and upstage his young partner with more long winded explanations. But he surprised me. Not a peep out of him. So I turned back to Bono and asked the obvious.

"Everyone who wins a major lottery is target for freeloaders, gets 'importuned' as you call it. You're suggesting there is more to it than that. What makes you think so?"

"Definitely there is more to it than that. We can deal with the regular vultures who turn up in these circumstances. But all of us, Chuck and Arthur here, Sonia of course, plus Betty Grelick—Sonia's old friend and agent, and Lew Davies—her arranger and coach, all of us feel sure that more than an ordinary problem many lottery winners face is involved. A systematic campaign against Sonia is what this is. And it must be stopped. It has scared her, she wants and needs protection, a body guard. That's the priority, of course. Making sure nothing actually happens to her. But also we need to get to the bottom of all this."

"All this—is what? What has actually happened?"

At this point Chuck Weller broke in. Unlike Sedgwick and Bono, there was little expensive polish about Sonia Deerfield's business manager, for that's who he turned out to be. Weller sported the long-suffering look and shining blue suit of a stereotypical small time bookkeeper. He chain-smoked a low tar and nicotine brand of cigarette and had the disconcerting habit of looking vaguely into space as if the goings on around him didn't hold his attention. Appearances can be very deceiving.

"I'll tell you," he said. "I was present for some of it. First, there've been threatening phone calls to Sonia's unlisted number. We changed the number and three days later he was back. The threats were vague, just a menacing male voice promising to 'get her' unless she turns money over to him. Nothing about how or who to. Then—"

I interrupted. "Have you told the cops? And Bell?" I looked first at Bono and then at Sedgwick. "Did you advise her that phone threats are a police matter? You two are her lawyers, isn't that right?"

"Well, yes and no." Bono had been expecting this question. "We handle her affairs, yes. And we told her that strictly speaking this is a police matter. But she refuses to involve the authorities. And, let's face it, publicity at this point wouldn't be advisable." He clearly wasn't comfortable with this answer but I let it go for the moment while Weller continued his story.

"Exactly. Sonia won't have any police or publicity about this. Even after other things started to happen. First her purse was snatched. Now, that could've been a coincidence except that the voice on the phone knew about it the same day. Then it got even more serious. Sonia's hotel suite was broken into— nothing taken, but her clothing and personal things disturbed. And again the caller mentioned it and threatened more of the same. Then she was almost knocked down by a car—"

"And you still didn't do anything? Weren't you taking a hell of a big risk?"

"Yes, yes. We're aware that the situation couldn't be allowed to continue. That's why we found you. Sonia wants a female bodyguard. She's heard of you and insisted we get you for the job. So you see, after the incident with the car, we had a meeting and decided that something had to be done and hiring someone like you was the best idea. So we got Burrows to find you and here we are."

"Since Sonia wanted me and she is the client, where is she now? Why isn't she here?" I thought I knew the answer to this question—these three men were checking me out to make sure I was suitable by their criteria to do the job. I was ready to bet that Sonia didn't even know about this meeting although it was her health and money which were under discussion. Only if I passed the test here would they produce me. Sedgwick was quick to see what was in my mind. He entered the conversation again.

"You see, Miss Keremos, it's a sensitive situation. Sonia Deer-field is a very talented singer at the threshold of a great career. She was just beginning to be noticed by people who matter in this business when she won the lottery. Up to this point most of her experience has been in clubs, private parties. Undoubtedly she'd made some unsavoury acquaintances. It is our opinion that it's someone from her past who sees an opportunity to profit from her good fortune. A major recording company is interested in her now and she has a chance at a legitimate concert- and recording-career. It would be foolhardy to endanger that. We must be careful with respect to any adverse publicity and whom we hire to investigate these unfortunate occurrences. I'm sure you see our problem."

"Sure. But I still want to meet the client and hear from her what has been happening and what she has in mind for me. And whom she suspects, of course. It surely hasn't escaped you that whoever is threatening her knows a great deal about her current life, must be close to her, have access to her? Some baddy from the past just won't do, you know. One of her 'friends' must be involved, in fact."

"Of course we realize it looks that way. But if you are implying that it's any one of us three or for that matter anyone else among her close friends and colleagues, well, I just can't believe it. But your job is to find out who is threatening Sonia, regardless of who it is." This was Ben Bono talking, vehemently.

I looked at Sedgwick who nodded his head. It struck me that more than business interest was involved in this whole operation. These two high-priced lawyers sounded like they cared too much. On the other hand Weller sat there and gave nothing away, staring straight in front of him. Altogether a strange situation. I decided to change the subject.

"What is it specifically that you want from me? You mentioned Sonia Deerfield's hotel suite. You want me to move there? I charge $200 per day plus expenses."

Bono answered, relief in his voice at what he took to be acceptance. "Yes, Sonia wants someone with her. There is an extra bedroom, you will be quite comfortable, and all expenses will be taken care of, naturally. Your fee is acceptable— no problem there. We want you to start right away. Sonia will be with Lew Davies, her arranger and coach, until 2 p.m. today. We could meet you at her suite then. Give you time to get your things."

"Not so fast. I want to see her first, alone. Give me the address, I'll be there at two this afternoon. After I've talked with her I'll let you know whether I'll take the job or not. Take it or leave it."

After a certain amount of grumbling and backtalk they agreed. The address I was given was of a hotel which had just been tarted up and made semi-respectable. It was convenient, central but not a great address or very expensive. Sonia Deerfield hadn't made it into the big time yet. They were keeping her under wraps, certainly money couldn't be the problem. A millionaire could afford something better than the Imperial Palace Hotel on Jarvis Street.

I left, promising to call Sedgwick's office later that afternoon after talking with Sonia. On my way down on the elevator and uptown to my borrowed apartment I mulled over the company around Sonia Deerfield. What was a smalltime singer—"clubs and private parties"—doing with such high-powered legal help before she won all that cash? I doubted that Sedgwick and Company had many clients in her category. Corporations and old, big money, that would be more their style. Not flaky show-biz types. And Weller. He didn't seem right for the part. In my experience business managers on the pop and rock music scene are loud, and obnoxiously full of themselves. Hype goes with the territory. Weller came across as too low key to qualify. He and Sedgwick knew each other too well; he wasn't in Sedgwick's league. More like a poor relation. Yet all three of these men—Sedgwick, Bono and Weller—were very tight. Like old cronies. It would bear checking into. Suddenly I realized that I was thinking as if it was a foregone conclusion I would take this case.

4

Any doubts about taking on the case disappeared as soon as I saw and spoke to Sonia Deerfield. I'd always been a sucker for red-heads; and Sonia's head blazed with thick, long, copper-red hair the colour of an Irish setter's. That alone wouldn't have been enough to make me take notice. She also had a quality of repressed tension which spoke volumes about the stress she was under and the control she had to exercise over herself just to function. Her control was perfect, much too perfect. She felt vulnerable and no amount of control could quite hide it. Certainly, if she wanted my help she could have it.

Sonia Deerfield walked quickly across the room towards me, wrapped in a long, soft gown. She looked at me directly and started without preliminaries.

"You are Helen. Helen Keremos. My friend Sally Richmond in Vancouver told me all about you. I would've known you anywhere. And you are just who I need. Oh, I'm so glad you're here. Now I'll be able to sleep nights. Can you move in right away?" Instead of green, her eyes looked almost yellow. I stopped her as she was about to go on.

"Hold on, hold on. Now, sit down and tell me all about it. What's been happening around here? What do you want from me other than just being here with you?"

"Yes, of course." There was a light sprinkling of freckles on her face and neck. She grinned self-deprecatingly, sat down, tucked her robe around her knees and continued. "It's difficult. My life in the past year or so has been so hectic, so many changes."

"Past year?" I wanted her to go back and be specific so I could make sense of the situation.

"Yes, yes. About a year ago things started to happen, good things I mean. My career started to take off. Suddenly I was getting better gigs. Nothing really big yet, you understand, not stardom, but better. You know, from tacky taverns to trendy

downtown rooms, to opening for a star act at Massey Hall."
She grinned again. "Chuck Weller as business manager. Two
record companies interested in me. And all so fast! Lawyers,
accountants. D'you know I'm incorporated now! Wow! I was
going places but, well, it all felt out of control somehow. You
know what I mean. I just wasn't used to it. All these people
around. Giving advice, making decisions for me. It didn't seem
like my life any more. I got interviewed. Articles in the *Star*
and *Toronto Life* called me 'new talent', although I'd been
working for years. All the hype, on and on. Yet I still didn't
have any money and nothing really firm.

"Then I won this million dollars. Well! At first it was like a
dream come true. I could afford to hold out for the best.
Better gigs and contracts. I can afford Lew Davies full time.
He's great. And we're putting together a great backup group
for me. Demo tapes and live gigs. Maybe a video. And I can
afford to negotiate with record companies, not have to take
whatever they choose to offer. So—" She stopped and fell
silent for a moment. Then she turned to me and continued
in a different tone. "Yet it doesn't feel right. The money only
speeds things up, makes it harder still to know what the hell
is going on. I'm less and less comfortable with my life. I
would've coped, you know, in spite of all that, but then these
phone calls! These threats, that voice on the phone, robbery,
'an accident'." Sonia shivered. "It's too much. I can't seem to
handle myself any more. I want out! I want it all to stop. All
of it. But there are all these plans, people dependent on me,
my career. Unless these threats stop I'll have a breakdown, I
can feel it. I'll go nuts." She looked away. "I don't really have
anyone, not really. Oh, there's Betty, and Ben and those others.
They are all very supportive and all that. But I still feel alone."

"No current lover, no family, no intimate friend?" I asked.
She took her time replying.

"I was married, you know, for a while. Walt and I split up
a couple of years ago. We are friendly, there isn't any hard
feeling between us. But Walt never was much use. And now
there is Ben. Ben Bono. We see each other, he wants to marry

me but I'm not sure. It's too complicated. He's my lawyer; part of the whole business. Both he and Arthur Sedgwick want to make me a big star, get us all into big time show biz. Now Ben says he will look after me, make sure nobody cheats me or hurts me. Yet neither Ben nor Arthur seem able to deal with this ghastly caller. Sometimes I just wish that none of this had happened, so I could be the old me. In the old days I saw friends, I knew the scene. Sure, we were all poor and all scrambling for a buck as best we could. But I was happier. Sounds corny but it's true. Now I don't know what's happening around me. Helen, I need help. Those threats are the last straw. It's not that I am afraid for my life or even my money. It's the pressure, and not knowing who is doing this to me and what they want. I'm getting jumpy, hate to be alone, can't sleep nights. I didn't use to be a mess like this. I consider myself a pretty together person. Look at me now! Will you stay and help me out? Please."

So who could refuse? "Sure. You've just hired me. I'll move in tonight. Now tell me in detail all about these 'incidents'. Everything you can remember."

Sonia's story didn't differ materially from what I had heard that morning in Sedgwick's office. A week after her win was made public she began to get calls. A man's voice threatening her with unspecified disasters, and demanding a share of her winnings. She got a new answering service, changed her phone number. The calls kept on. She wanted the answering service to stop taking messages but Ben had insisted they continue.

"He's right, you know," I said. "In the first place, it helps to know what's in the caller's head. Secondly, if you cut him off there he is more likely to try something else, something worse than phone calls. He probably will sooner or later, anyway."

"That's what Ben said. We finally decided, no, I insisted, that we get a woman detective to handle it. And to be with me. It will be good to have a strong woman around," she added wistfully. Sonia sure knew how to manipulate her audience, especially a susceptible one like me. I was being set up and loving it. It didn't matter that I knew it. Sonia was in real

— 19 —

trouble and needed real help. All this heart-warming stuff she was dishing out didn't make her situation any the less authentically difficult.

"So you have no close friends you can turn to outside this lot. How about family?" Give me credit, I was trying to get on with it, concentrate on the essentials. It was time to get busy sorting out this mess. Feelings had to wait.

"My parents are both dead. I've a sister, June. She's married to a rancher in Alberta." Sonia giggled, remembering. For a moment I saw what she might be like without the weight of problems on her shoulders. It didn't help my objectivity. She went on: "She met him at a Grey Cup party, you know what those football fans are like. She and I had been hired to entertain part of the western contingent. God, but these guys were awful pigs! Anyway, June stayed with this rancher, cowboy boots and all. He went home but what-do-you-know, he came back to Toronto and took her to Alberta with him. They're all properly married now of course, and have turned into religious and political fundamentalists, to make matters worse. Too 'holier than thou' for me. I sent June a gift when I got my winnings—she is my only sister—but they don't need my money and don't approve of me." She didn't sound sorry. "Then there is my Uncle Karl in Owen Sound. He runs a service station and calls me once in a while."

"What about your ex?"

"Walt? Well, it wasn't a great marriage and he isn't a respectable citizen. Arthur and Ben would like to believe it's Walt who's doing the calling, but they won't admit it. I think it's because they don't know anyone like him so it looks likely to them. But he wouldn't do anything like this to me. Walt is OK."

"Do you suspect someone, anyone at all? Someone from your past, someone with a grudge?"

"No." But she didn't sound sure. "Not really. I've known a lot of people and some of them, like Walt, could be considered pretty flaky. I'm sure I've made some enemies too. Envy is a powerful emotion. But I can't think of anyone in particular, no."

I didn't leave Sonia's apartment until almost 4 p.m., going over and over the events of the last year and especially the month just past. I got a lot of detail but nothing immediately useful. I called Sedgwick's office and told the super efficient secretary that I was taking the case. Finally I left, having promised Sonia that I'd be back with my toothbrush by 7:30 to have dinner with her, Betty Grelick and Lew Davies—two people I was very interested to meet.

5

THAT AFTERNOON I went about my business, phoned people, called in some I.O.U.s. Then I went to see Alex Edwards. She and I had worked together on the Martin Millwell case some years previously. I'd stayed at her place then and we were looked upon as 'an item'. In fact, we'd never become lovers, primarily because we didn't want to complicate our friendship with an affair. Until five weeks ago I'd been away, latterly working on a case in Washington D.C.

When I got back to Toronto, Alex was busy and hard to reach. When we did finally meet I decided against moving into her life again. She understood perfectly well why I preferred to sit in a borrowed apartment rather than share her cozy little house in the Beaches but she was miffed about it none the less. None of which interfered any with our respect and love for each other and our mutual pleasure at working together again. I told her the gist of the Sonia Deerfield story; Alex was unimpressed and sceptical. My 'unprofessional' interest in Sonia did not pass unnoticed.

"Hey, hey. What's this? Sure, a case is a case and it's nice working where there's money for a change. But why waste time and sympathy on a millionaire with expensive legal talent in her corner? Poor little rich girl's in trouble. So what? You're getting soft in your old age, or what? Most likely it's her ex-husband, with one of the insiders helping him. No big deal. You're supposed to be going back west. Sort it out fast and be on your way. Just don't get involved. $200 per day ain't so much." This from Alex who lives on about $15,000 a year, volunteers at a community newspaper and does more work for peanuts or for free than any three other women I know.

"Your confidence in my abilities is touching. I don't think it's all quite that simple. Now, don't you worry your pretty little head about money. Remember you're an expense. As for 'so what?'—you haven't met Sonia. She's no self-pitying rich kid. And we can't even be sure that Sedgwick and his lot are really in her corner. Could be quite the reverse. She needs help and she can also afford to pay for it, what could be a better arrangement?"

"Well, just be sure she's not after your body beautiful. Or you hers," Alex laughed, sharp as ever. I made no comment so she went on, "Seriously, I'm glad you're on a case again. You're always better company when you're working. Last time I saw you you were mad enough to spit nails about just about everything. Now look at you, full of piss and vinegar!"

"Yeah, it's good to be working again, especially with you. Even if it does postpone my trip home. So let's get down to cases. First of all, get that electronic whiz buddy of yours—what's his name, Peter—to come to the hotel tomorrow first thing and check Sonia's suite for bugs. Someone is getting information about her which isn't in the gossip columns. You're right, it's probably coming via one of these insiders but let's just remove all other possibilities. OK. Then start in on Sedgwick, Bono, Weller, Grelick, Davies and Sonia's ex-husband Walter Lauker. And of course Sonia herself. I want all you can get asap."

"Thanks a lot. And what shall I do in my spare time?"

"Complain, what else," I retorted. "All you can get by tomorrow afternoon. So get on it."

Alex is, rightly, proud of her connections, her ability to turn up information, find the right source and make sudden and unlikely arrangements. She lives with impossible deadlines and pressure doesn't faze her a bit. Like most of us she likes to have her skills appreciated and valued. She knows I know that she is the best in her field and believes that I am pretty good in mine. We make a good team. As we bantered, she sat happily making notes and mumbling half to herself, half to me. Then she got to work seriously.

"Right then. 'Get Peter re: bugs'. He might not be free tomorrow a.m., you know. Can't expect everyone to drop everything else they are doing just on your say-so."

"Not on my say-so, on yours. Just say it's important and tell him we'll pay commercial rates, not community rates. He'll come through."

"OK. Sedgwick, Sedgwick, Arthur Sedgwick. Don't know him. But if he is the big shot you describe he won't be hard to get a bead on. Betty Grelick I've heard of. She runs a small booking agency, Bloor Street area, she's in the scene. Now Weller, is he a lawyer too?"

"Don't know. He sure doesn't look smooth enough but anything is possible. He was described as Sonia's business manager. Doesn't look or act like one of those jerks either. More like a Central Casting underpaid bookkeeper."

"Oh, it can't be! It must be! I remember now. There was a Weller, a lawyer who got disbarred. I saw him on TV, could it be him?"

"Weller a disbarred lawyer? It could be. Would account for the connection with Sedgwick and the way Weller brown-nosed him. What's the point of speculating? Find out about him."

"Yeah, him and six others, or is it seven? You don't want much by tomorrow, do you! And what will you be doing while I do all this leg work for you?"

"Phone work, if I know anything about the way you operate. Bet you never leave the house. As to what I'll be doing, well, hanging out with a beautiful millionaire is what. Eat your heart out."

"A tough assignment, I know. While you're hanging out in posh hotels, drinking champagne cocktails or whatever, take a minute from making time with this Sonia woman and give Nate Ottoline a call. He knows the music scene inside out. And he will tell you more than he'll tell me."

"I'm way ahead of you. I've called him already and left a message with Ronnie. Remember Ronnie? And I'm having a private, unlisted phone put into Sonia's suite in my name. Should be in tomorrow. Use that if you have to call me. No extensions. Sonia's phone has three; one in every room. Plus the house phone. Great place to keep secrets."

"You're getting a new phone in twenty-four hours? How did you manage that?"

"Pull, what else."

"Pull with Papa Bell! That's almost unheard of for a mere mortal. You have to be a big subscriber. How d'you do it?"

"Sonia's hotel is part of a big chain. And I happen to know Chester, the house dick there. He owes me. Naturally a chain like that can get service ordinary people only dream of. The phone will be in tomorrow, never fear. Incidentally, Chester already suspected something fishy was going on with their pet tenant. Not much gets by a pro like him. Anyway, he's keeping an eye on things for me. Like comings and goings to and from that suite. No harm having that covered. Meet with your approval so far?"

"Not bad. You have been working. Just keep it professional. OK, now get the hell out of here so I can get to work."

6

WHEN I GOT to the Imperial Palace Hotel, Chester, my tame house dick, met me in the lobby with news.

"Listen Helen, there was a man hanging around here this afternoon, late. He used the house phone to call the Deerfield suite. I don't know who he spoke to but I happened to overhear his end of the conversation. Interested?"

"Depends who he was. If it was a pest exterminator arranging to chase cockroaches, then no, I'm not interested. Give me a break, don't waste my time."

"Now, now. No cracks about my place of employment. In this establishment most of the vermin have two legs and it's my job to deal with them. This guy gave his name as Walt. And he made a date with whoever he spoke with for tonight, at his, Walt's place. This visit is to take place between two and four a.m. Strange time, eh? That's why I thought you might be interested." This 'Walt' had to be Walter Lauker, Sonia's ex-husband. Another party heard from. This case was getting crowded.

"OK, that's worth a drink. Who was up there at the time, do you know?"

"Not for sure. There was a whole bunch of them in the suite. Most of the usual crowd. We tend to notice strangers not regulars, you know. Two have left since then; Bono the Wop lawyer and that sad case, Weller. The rest, a couple I think, are still there so you can go up and check for yourself."

"Thanks for the tip. Keep working."

"If that was worth just one drink, what do I have to do to get out of hock with you? Don't answer that, I can guess. OK, OK, I'll keep my eyes open for you. Anything to help a fellow gum-shoe. Be careful." He blew cigarette smoke in my face and marched off. Hotel security people are not the nicest folks in the world. The job doesn't pay much, the hours are horrible and there is nowhere to go but down. So naturally, most of them are out to see what they can organize on the side. Chester owed me a favour which he would try to repay; sure, but he wasn't likely to let any opportunity to make a buck slip by him. That was understood.

I took the elevator to the sixth floor and knocked at the door of Sonia's suite instead of using my key. A short, dark man in rumpled recycled clothes opened the door. His voice had a pleasant Welsh lilt to it. Davies.

"You're Helen, right? Hello. Come in, come in. I'm Lew Davies, Sonia's chief gofer and bottle washer. Sometimes coach and arranger, as well."

"Hi, Lew," I said and looked around the room at Sonia and another woman who had to be Betty Grelick. Sonia, still in her robe, waved a cocktail glass at me. Betty Grelick was a blond, carefully made-up woman in expensive, funky clothes. She poured herself a glass of wine at the well stocked bar and smiled at me encouragingly, like a star at a backward adolescent fan.

"I'm Betty Grelick." She didn't elaborate. I nodded politely to acknowledge them all, accepted a drink from Lew Davies and sat down waiting for the conversation to pick up. Which it did immediately. None of the three paid any attention to me as they plunged back into it. They had a way, common to old friends in the same business, of all speaking at once, yet hearing and understanding each other perfectly. Since there were virtually no pauses it was impossible for any fourth party to get a word in edgewise. I didn't try, just let them run on. The room filled with their nervous energy stimulated by good booze and the implications brought home by my presence. They loudly discussed gigs past and current, good and bad; recording studios and the vagaries of A&R men; various night spots where Sonia had worked; idiosyncracies of club owners, band members and back-up singers; waiters, customers and other performers. It was a totally in-group conversation carried on as if I wasn't there. It shut out everyone else and anything else which was on their minds. Like the threats to Sonia. In among the quips, the comments and the jokes a picture of Sonia's life emerged—hectic, even frantic, exciting and totally one dimensional. Sonia's career and success in the music scene absorbed them all to the exclusion of all else. Her success, current and to be, was the success of the other two; identification was complete.

Dinner was sent in. We ate chicken and salad followed by a Dufflet torte. We drank wine, coffee and liqueurs. The fringe benefits of this case were not to be sneezed at. Somewhere in all the chatter the reason for my presence among them surfaced. First Walt Lauker's name came up; all of them denied having had any recent contact with him. Then Sonia's Uncle Karl was mentioned. It seems that he wanted to move in with Sonia to guide and protect her. Sonia should have a member of her family around to help out at this trying moment. That was the idea. Betty approved of it, feeling that it would be more 'appropriate' than having a detective/bodyguard, like me. I got the distinct impression that Betty wasn't very keen on me. She had apparently deferred to the opinion of the three absent men—Sedgwick, Bono and Weller—but was not herself convinced that I was necessary or would do any good. But it was Sonia who put her foot down in no uncertain manner.

"I don't want Uncle Karl. This requires a professional and Helen is just the person. I'm going to enjoy having her around." That's exactly what was bugging Betty. It wasn't clear however whether she resented me specifically or just any woman who might get close to Sonia.

"Yes, well. I'm sure Helen is very competent, no offence and all that, Helen, but family is family, you know." Betty's hostility was rather thinly veiled. Sonia ignored the issue. For her the matter was closed.

Lew Davies appeared to have missed these little by-plays. He was cheerful, pleasant, and helpful. In his role as general dog's-body for Sonia he supplied me with everyone's address; offered help and advice; filled me in on details of Sonia's busy schedule. Without being too obvious about it he and I arranged to cover Sonia's days between us so she wouldn't be alone. After all, if I was to do any detecting I couldn't be bodyguarding her twenty-four hours a day. So I was to have next day from twelve noon to four p.m. to go about my business. Sonia would be with Lew Davies at lunch and rehearsing. It was wonderful to watch the adroit way in which Lew handled those arrangements. It takes practice and just the right personality to manage people with the skill he was displaying. Lew was an experienced operator. It never became too obvious that I was being manipulated into accepting him as an ally rather than as someone who was, after all, a suspect.

An interesting evening. Sometimes you learn more from what people do not say than what they do say. By the time Lew Davies and Betty Grelick had left and Sonia and I had said goodnight and gone to our respective rooms, one fact was shrieking out at me. Throughout the whole evening that the four of us had been together Sonia's million had barely been mentioned.

7

AT ONE FORTY-FIVE a.m. that morning I sat well back behind the wheel of my new truck parked outside Walt Lauker's home on a side street in mid-town Toronto. It hadn't been easy to get myself up and out. Sonia was sound asleep when I left the suite. I hated to leave her alone but there was no real alternative. The best I could do as I tiptoed out was to check with Chester and the sleepy clerk on duty at the desk. Then I drove the unfamiliar, new-smelling truck through the all-night mid-town traffic to Lauker's. He lived in an old house recently converted into 'bachelorettes'. There were six bells at the door. Since his apartment was number one it was probably on the ground floor. All the downstairs windows were dark; the only light came from the third floor. He was out or asleep or watching TV. There was nothing for it but to park with a good view of the house and settle down to wait for the mysterious visitor to arrive.

Night stake-outs like this can be a real bore. But the Annex, a desirable residential area just north of the University of Toronto's midtown campus, is a more interesting place to be stuck in than most. Group homes, remains of counter-culture organizations of various types sit cheek by jowl with fraternity houses and offices of trendy lawyers. It houses a motley crew of students, artists, media freelancers, fringe 'professionals' who are rapidly being displaced by both new and old wealth. Here, there is still life after 2 a.m. Groups of young people go by, their voices alive with beer and sexual excitement. A couple wrestles in a parked car. A single pedestrian passes slowly, shoulders hunched against the night air.

By two thirty the street was empty of pedestrian traffic. The only action was the odd taxi discharging a fare at a dark house or a private car searching for a nonexistent parking space on the block. At two forty-eight a large white and red Post Office step van rattled past on its lawful rounds. A yellow police cruiser wheeled quietly along the street, its inside light on, reflecting on the cops' crewcut necks, hatless against regulations. Soon after, a tired-looking black man in a hire-a-cop uniform drove past with his CB radio buzzing. More taxis. Some drove fast, barely pausing at the cross streets; others crawled along looking for a house number, backing up to check and finally disgorging their weary passengers and pulling slowly, almost reluctantly away.

At three fifteen a.m. cramp in my left leg makes me wish I was back in bed. I keep having to rearrange my 5'9" on the still unfamiliar seat. I regret giving up smoking. To keep my mind active and fight sleep I force myself to think back to similar occasions in the past. How often have I sat in a parked car at night watching an empty street? Too often; dozens of times. I try recalling each instance and put it in context of the case but they all run together. All I can remember are degrees of discomfort and boredom; dreary nights which lead nowhere seem no different than dreary nights which produce results and solve cases.

Suddenly out of an empty street comes a white Volvo station wagon. It rolls past on silent wheels, climbs the curb and stops, half blocking the sidewalk opposite Walt Lauker's house. I snap wide awake. A dark-coated figure gets out of the Volvo, crosses the street and runs up the steps to Lauker's front door. A bell is pressed and almost immediately the door opens automatically. Under the hall light the pleasant Celtic features of Lew Davies show up clearly for a second. As the door closes behind him a light comes on downstairs in a room with the big bay window. Bingo! Sonia's faithful friend and coach is about to have a secret confab with her ex-husband. Sneaky buggers.

Davies arrived at three eighteen a.m. to see Lauker by the latter's invitation. An invitation extended over the house phone at Sonia's hotel. But why? I had to get my mind in gear; this didn't make any sense. Why not call Davies at home? Why take a chance, risk a trip to the hotel? There was only one explanation that I could see. The call had been made to Sonia, the house phone was the only way to contact her without going through the switchboard and the answering service. Why then did Lew Davies show up at Lauker's? Again the answer was obvious. Sonia had sent him. I began to speculate on the relationship between these three.

Before I could get very far in my speculations, Davies ran out of the house slamming the door behind him. He ran across to the white car and pulled away in the space of seconds. My dashboard clock displayed the figures three twenty-four a.m. in bright green. Just a six minute visit. Not long enough for anything much. I stared at the curtained windows. The light remained on. I didn't like the look of Davies' hurried exit. Muttering under my breath I got my gun from under the seat and walked quickly over to the house. Suspicion is a detective's occupational disease. Six minutes is not long enough to do much business, to discuss, explain or persuade, but it's plenty long enough to kill. And three a.m. is the perfect time for it.

8

I PUSHED THE BUZZER marked 'Apt. #1–Lauker' in elaborate script. As I started to reach into my pocket for my handy-dandy lock picking kit, the door clicked open. I stepped into the hall, looked around me and turned left. The door of Apartment 1 stood open. Even before it shut behind me I knew that my murder scenario was dead wrong. There was the sizzle and smell of frying. In the dim light a man holding a frypan stared at me across the cluttered room. He looked about thirty, medium build, nondescript brown hair a bit shaggy, face pale and a pair of the bluest eyes you ever saw this side of Robert Redford. I put away my gun, feeling sheepish.

Walter Lauker was fully dressed, if you can call it that, in dirty black peg-leg pants, a belted smoking jacket in red and black plaid with a full shawl collar over a shirtless body, odd socks—one black, one brown—and a pair of genuine carpet slippers, the kind that haven't been made for years. We stared at each other in mutual surprise.

"Oh!" he said. "I thought you were someone else."

"Lew Davies? He left. You're Walter Lauker, right?"

"At your service. I thought maybe Lew forgot something. Now you are here, join me in a bite to eat? Don't usually have company with my meals." He turned back casually to the hot plate and stirred the mess in the pan. Cool. I surveyed the room. It had been the main, formal livingroom, probably originally called 'drawing room', when this house had been the family home of a wealthy merchant back in the twenties. Now it was split-up and transformed into expensive and desirable little flats. Much of its charm remained. High ceiling, plentifully embellished with plaster medallions. An imposing fireplace, now sadly inoperative. Beautiful bay windows with built-in window seats. Solid oak door which once opened to what was the back hall now led into a small bathroom. Next to this door and opposite the windows was a small refrigerator and the hot plate at which my host stood imperturbably.

The large room was completely full. At first glance all that I saw was the outer layer. Every available surface was covered with what appeared to be junk. Old magazines, discarded clothes, china, bric-a-brac, tools, books, garden ornaments, an indescribable assortment of odds and sods. A particularly ugly plaster flamingo with a chipped wing rivetted my attention. I tore my gaze from its beady eyes and realised that under the obvious mess the room was solid with furniture. Wall to wall. Pieces that looked like antiques and stuff that might pass for antiques in a plastic world. Cupboards, chests and chairs; benches, bureaus and beds; stools, sofas and sideboards. And tables. Lots of tables; I counted six of various shapes and sizes. One enormous roll top desk probably worth a small fortune. I looked up from contemplating these treasures to find Lauker watching me, deadpan.

"Thanks, yes, I'll stay and have a cup of coffee," I said. A slow smile spread over his face.

"Good." He turned back to the hot plate, turned it off, picked up a coffee pot, two mugs, put them down on a pile of old *Connoisseur* magazines and poured the coffee. "Find a chair," he continued, picking up one of the mugs and perching on the edge of the unmade bed. I cleared a cracked soup tureen and a rusty auger from a half-stripped pine kitchen chair, got the other mug and sat down. We looked at each other.

"Pleasedtomeecha." Lauker spoke first, grinning over the rim of his mug. He knew who I was, that was clear.

"Likewise," I answered, going along with the game. "You work at this. And you are good at it."

"I work at whatever I do and I'm good at whatever I do."

"Likewise. Did you work at being married to Sonia Deerfield?"

"Oh, my. Are the preliminaries over already? Pity. Yes, I worked at it. Sonia didn't."

"And what are you working at now? Besides being eccentric that is."

"Nothing. Just that. Takes all my time."

"Indeed. Doesn't it get boring? Without an audience, I mean."

"On the contrary. I like working alone until I'm perfect. It's the artist in me, I guess."

"And once you're perfect—?"

"Then I get an audience. No problem. They come in droves. It's so rare nowadays to find someone who really has the talent for eccentricity. So it's trendy. Case of supply and demand, you know." He would have prattled on but I interrupted.

"And then you do your number or unfold your scenario or whatever you call it. Yes, I see. Well, thanks for the coffee. Goodnight." I rose. It was 4 a.m. and I wasn't in any mood to feed him straight lines.

"Hey! You can't do that. We aren't finished yet. Aren't there more questions you want to ask me?" He was obviously keen on keeping me there to practise his patter on. To find out more about me, perhaps. So far he had handled himself with style given that my arrival was totally unexpected. He had guessed who I was from what Lew Davies had told him only a few minutes previously. Walter Lauker was pretty fast on his feet. My tactic was to play hard to get. So I said:

"Not much point when I know the answers. Lew Davies was here a while ago, he told you I'd been hired, and described me. What else? Oh, yes, he also brought you a cheque from Sonia. It's plainly visible on that desk. $500 made out to you. No, I don't think I have any more questions right now. Goodnight again."

"Don't you want to know if I'm the phantom caller?" He was slipping.

"Are you?"

"No, not my style at all." He grasped the opening but I wouldn't let him continue.

"Right. So there you are. 'Bye."

"Oh, OK, OK. You're a spoil sport, you know." He was smiling again, acknowledging that he'd been out-maneuvered. "But you don't know as much as you think. For instance, this cheque. Look at it more closely." I picked it up. It was Sonia's personal cheque drawn on a trust company.

"What about it?" I asked.

"That's the million dollar account. Doesn't it give you a thrill? To be that close to a million dollars," Lauker teased.

"Not particularly. There aren't enough zeros on this cheque. Are you trying to tell me that Sonia keeps the whole bundle in a simple chequing account? Didn't Sedgwick or somebody invest it for her?" Lauker was happy to have gotten a bite. He waved his coffee mug excitedly.

"No, no. That's just it! Sedgwick and his crew never got their mits on any of it, although they carry on as if they had. Sonia deposited it in this account immediately after her win and now acts as if it didn't exist. Except for a small donation to yours truly, of course." He watched for my reaction. Both of us understood the possibilities this opened up. The absurd harassment campaign now made much more sense. If Lauker was right, then all the phantom caller had to do was to work on Sonia's nerve ends until she couldn't stand it any more and signed a cheque. No lawyers, accountants, brokers need be involved. No opportunity for discussion and dissuasion. Sonia could remove the pressure from herself by the simple and familiar act of signing a cheque. A cheque just like this one. I looked at Walter Lauker.

"Interesting if true. It does kind of make you the prime suspect, doesn't it?"

"A suspect, yes. But one among many."

"Maybe. But the prime suspect. What's this lousy five hundred dollars for? Blackmail payment? A dry run for the big pay-off?"

"You disappoint me. Blackmail? If I'd something on Sonia and wanted to blackmail her, harassment wouldn't be necessary, now would it? And what's the sense of a measly five hundred dollars, anyway?"

"Exactly. To most simple minds it wouldn't make any sense. But for you—it just might. Let's suppose that in spite of your denials and your honest face you are Sonia's harasser. You could have a number of motives. Revenge for leaving you. Showing your power over her life. Putting a spoke in the wheels of Sedgwick and the other boys. A quick pay-off isn't in your character. You would want to prolong the fun. You would like the game for its own sake. Big money could come later. Well, how am I doing so far?" As I spoke, Lauker held himself very still. He needed to work on his body language. It can be a dead give away.

"No. Believe me or not, as you please, but no. I'm not interested in harassing my ex-wife. And this five hundred and others like it are unsolicited gifts from Sonia. For old time's sake. No blackmail, no harassment. Not me. Not my style." For a moment it was difficult to figure whether his seriousness was bluff or double bluff. Or double-double bluff. Was it one more ploy in his private game, or had he actually suspended the game altogether?

"All right. Let's assume you're a lily white innocent. Not an easy assumption to make but let's look at the alternatives. Who's your candidate?" I asked Lauker. Immediately he brightened.

"Thought you'd never ask. My bet's on Betty Grelick and Chuck Weller in the villain roles. Independently or in combination." He looked expectant.

"I'll bite. Why?" I said, taking the bait.

"Many reasons. You're the detective, you find out."

So he'd told me all he wanted me to know, he'd had his fun and now I was getting the push. In spite of myself, I was annoyed.

"Coyness doesn't become you. That's what I'm doing now, detecting. And I'd much rather be asleep in bed. If you have something to say, say it now. You may enjoy the sound of your own voice all night but I don't."

The level of our dialogue, if it could be called that, had deteriorated markedly.

"I'll give you a hint. Or two. First of all both Grelick and Weller need money. And neither are quite what they seem," he said.

"So who is? Is that all you've got? Big deal. A million dollars is a motive for anyone, needing money doesn't make it special. How about a little means and opportunity for either of them? Something concrete to tie them in, I mean." It didn't work.

"That's all. At least that's all I'm going to tell you. Now do your own dirty work. Let's see how good you are."

"You're one sweet man." I got up and made my way out through the chaos of the room.

On my way back to Sonia's suite and my lonely bed I couldn't help thinking that Lauker's performance for my benefit was fully in character with that of the phantom caller. Providing tidbits of information, on how easy it was to get at the million—was that correct, I wondered—throwing a couple of names at me and then clamming up when I showed interest. These were actions not unlike those of the harasser who had also been mysterious, making no specific demands, giving no instructions. No sums of money had ever been mentioned. It seemed pointless trouble making, just for the fun of it, a way of getting attention. That was Lauker to a T, on the surface at least. There were a couple of points where the profiles didn't quite match. One was the anonymity. It was hard to imagine Lauker keeping up a long term consistent campaign of this kind without taking personal 'credit' for it. Would he get enough jollies just watching—presumably vicariously via Lew Davies—the effect he was having? Wouldn't he need to be recognized and acknowledged? The other point which didn't jibe was the relationship between Sonia Deerfield and Walter Lauker. It's not unknown for ex-spouses to do horrible things to each other. In fact, it's par for the course. But these two seemed genuinely on the best of terms. There was no hint of any bitterness between them. And that is something which is hard to hide. Which left Lauker with little that was obvious in the way of motive.

By the time I got to bed I was too tired to worry at these questions any further. I put the subject of Lauker himself on hold and fell asleep thinking of Betty Grelick and Charles Weller. Just as Lauker had intended.

9

JUST A COUPLE OF HOURS LATER I was up again. That morning was no time to hold any serious discussions with my client about her ex or anything else. Sonia's apartment was a zoo. First Peter the de-bugging whiz showed up. By eight thirty he was going over the place like a burglar checking for unauthorized electronic surveillance. Peter is the silent type; besides, he wore earphones the whole time he was with us, so conversation was minimal. He barely said hello, did his thing, gave the place a clean bill of health and split. By the time our breakfast arrived so had the installer from the phone company. One of those handsome, muscled types who view themselves as Pa Bell's gift to women. This one must have been fairly sophisticated because, after a long look at Sonia and me at breakfast together he quit flexing his biceps at us and had my phone installed in no time at all.

Sonia had a quick coffee and went to shower so I tried getting Nate Ottoline again on my new line. Nate and I had met during the Millwell case. He is a sharp business operator in the music, entertainment and gay scenes in this city. He owns a couple of after-hours clubs, and has interests in a number of flaky areas on both sides of the law. Together with Ronnie, his social secretary, sexual partner and butler, Nate became a trusted friend before the Millwell case was over. He was a natural source of information on Sonia Deerfield and her entourage. But I'd no luck again. Ronnie told me Nate was out of town. Ronnie himself had never heard of Sonia Deerfield but promised to check around and call back. That was the best I could do at the moment.

While Sonia was dressing her phone rang. I answered it before the answering service could cut in. It was Betty Grelick and surprise, she wanted to talk to me. Could she have lunch with me? If I wasn't too busy. I said sure. How about meeting at her office just off Bloor Street at 1:15, she suggested. I said sure.

Sonia appeared. She wore grey pants and a green sweater. Her gorgeous hair was combed back out of the way. Having bowled me over at our first meeting to get me to work for her, she was now subdued and rather uncomfortable with me. The previous night, with Davies and Grelick in attendance, we had hardly spoken to each other. This morning all we had managed were the usual breakfast courtesies. There was no opportunity for any more since both of us had full schedules. Sonia was due for her practice session. I got a cab and we drove in silence to Davies' sand-blasted old house in Cabbagetown. Sonia got out without a word and walked up the steps. As I watched, Davies opened the door and waited for her on the stoop. That was that. I gave the taxi driver Alex's address in the Beaches.

There wasn't any information for me at Alex's yet. She was expecting call-backs on half a dozen inquiries she'd set in motion since I'd seen her last. She assured me that someone among her extensive stable of contacts would come through with the real poop on Sedgwick and the others. There was nothing to do but wait.

We drank coffee and talked. Tactfully, Alex didn't tease me about Sonia this time. Instead, I regaled her with the tales of last night's events like my dinner with Betty Grelick, Lew Davies and Sonia. Of course, what she liked best was the story of my encounter with Walt Lauker. I made it as colourful as possible. Alex was enchanted. She tends to be a back-room sort of worker seldom in the midst of things herself. While not personally exposed to the outside world a lot she digs hearing about new people, tricky situations and small victories. As for me, having someone I trust with whom to talk over the job is very useful, not to mention pleasant.

The phone finally began to ring shortly before noon. By the time I left for my lunch with Betty Grelick I knew that Chuck Weller was indeed a disbarred lawyer, that Arthur Sedgwick had a reputation as an art collector in addition to being a real legal heavy-weight with his finger in a great many profitable pies. There were also a few bits and pieces of music biz shop gossip about Sonia Deerfield, Betty Grelick and Lew Davies but nothing I could make anything of.

Betty Grelick has a small, tasteful office in a remodelled building just off fashionable Bloor Street West. She greeted me pleasantly, obviously having decided to be charming rather than resentful. Definitely an improvement. She was head-to-toe in tailored denim, a casually expensive French designer outfit with embroidered vest and good jewellery. If she was short of money, it wasn't showing. I was offered a drink and accepted. Betty mixed two powerful Bloody Marys. Then followed an awkward pause. Whatever the purpose of her lunch invitation now that I was there, she had trouble getting the situation organized to her liking.

"How long have you and Sonia been friends?" I asked tactfully. It was a safe opening. Got the ball rolling and allowed her to take the conversation in any direction she chose.

"Years. A long time. Since she got into the business. I got her her very first booking. We've been friends ever since."

"When did Weller join the party? How long has she had him as manager?"

"Weller only came along a year or so ago. Sonia never had a manager before then. Just an agent—me." Betty Grelick smiled wistfully and left it at that.

"So you are her oldest friend as well as business associate, is that right?" I asked.

"Sonia Deerfield is my best friend," she answered.

"I see."

"Do you? I hope so. It's not an easy position to be in, right now. And it's hard to talk about it to you, to explain to a stranger, without appearing petty, jealous, or greedy. Can you believe me when I say that my only concern is for Sonia? That I want what is best for her? That I don't care about these others—oh, what's the use!"

"Try me."

"Don't you see what a spot I'm in? If I say anything about any of it, her men, her career, it all sounds like sour grapes. They all make clucking noises whenever I comment on anything. Implying that I'm a bitchy female, jealous of their influence in Sonia's life. That I'm small time and resent that they are taking Sonia into the big time. But I don't care how successful she is! I mean I care... But I'm not sure. I'm glad she can afford a full-time manager and all those men, lawyers. If only I believed it was right for her. But it's not, you know. It doesn't feel right and I trust my instincts. And now this million dollars! It's all so horrible."

"By me, a million dollars ain't so horrible. But I get the picture. Suddenly Sonia is surrounded by new people who could do her a lot of good. Help her career. Maybe. So you're in no position to criticize. Anything you do say is used against you, you are made to seem small minded and envious. A tough situation. Especially since you can't be sure just what is good for Sonia these days. You can't win. Right?"

"Right. And now they hire you. Is that a good thing or not? I'm not sure. I know Sonia wants you around; I know she needs protection. But—"

"Easy. I've nothing to do with Sonia's career and all of that. I'm only after the sucker who is threatening her. That could be anybody. A million beans is one hell of a temptation."

"I guess so," she said.

"You guess so! Come on! Don't weird me out. You are just as bad as those guys downtown. Nobody is talking about that million and what it means. It's not natural. You're trying to ignore its existence altogether in spite of those threats, break-ins and accidents. And you're only going through the motions about them. As if neither the money nor the threats were real. As if the money was the problem rather than the threats. How come? You think you know who is responsible for those phone calls so you aren't taking them too seriously. That part I understand. But how come no interest in all that lovely dough? It just won't wash, you know."

"Yes, yes. I guess it does look strange. And yes, we mostly feel it's Walt playing one of his weird games. But he wouldn't actually hurt Sonia for real so we thought that the best way to deal with the whole matter was to ignore it. Why encourage him? He'll get bored and go on to something else."

"You hope. Shit, I can't believe it. In the first place you aren't sure that it's Walt, are you? And even if it is, you can't be sure he's all that harmless. It's one hell of a risky assumption."

"I know, I know. It's just that Lew and I have known Walt for years. It's the sort of thing he might get into. But he's OK really."

"What about Weller, Sedgwick and Bono? They can't be so sure Walt is just a living doll. They haven't known him for years."

"Lew and I explained to them the sort of a man Walter is. So they half believe it. Not quite, I guess."

"Not quite. That's right. Sedgwick wouldn't take your word that the sun rises in the east. Weller takes his orders from Sedgwick, right? That leaves Bono. What's with him?"

"Ben Bono's in love with Sonia. Wants her to marry him. Lately he's been very pressing. This trouble gives him extra ammunition. 'Marry me and I'll protect you and look after you' etc. etc. That's his line."

"Sonia isn't buying that, is she? How does she feel about Walter Lauker?" By now Betty and I had established a fragile connection. We spoke like fellow conspirators. I hoped it would last just a little longer.

"That's the trouble. Sonia is of two minds about everything these days. She freaked out when all this started. Now she half wishes it's Walt, half hopes it isn't. And this thing with Ben. She does, she doesn't; she will, she won't. It's like that about everything. Her uncle Karl from Owen Sound offered to move in with her, hold her hand sort of. But no, she won't have him. Says she doesn't need anyone. Then she insists Arthur get you. One day she cries and breaks down on my shoulder, next she acts like it's all a scam, fun and games, not worth a serious thought. That goes for everything; her career, her money, her men."

"And you? How do you stand with her?" I asked, knowing full well that I could lose her confidence over her relationship with Sonia.

"I told you, we're old friends and always will be. No matter what," Betty said defensively. And that was that. I suggested it was getting late for lunch. Betty picked up on this with evident relief.

"Oh, I'm sorry. Inviting you to lunch and then starving you. Let's go."

We got into her little BMW and she drove to one of those restaurants that are trying hard to be in and not quite making it. I couldn't help being amused by this tactic. The place was expensive and smart enough not to amount to a putdown, yet safely unfashionable so that no one who knew her would see us together.

Over her quiche she told me about Walter Lauker.

"He was a waiter in one of the joints Sonia worked in. She did everything in those days—including topless go-go dancing. But she could sing and outclassed all the other girls. Anyway Sonia and Walt met in this joint, I think they worked there for over a year. Never lived together but then one day they up and got married. At City Hall. Back to work the same night. Everyone was real surprised by the whole thing. We all thought Walt had done very well for himself. Sonia obviously had a future."

"It sounds like one of those showbiz movies of the thirties. All glamour and romance and no real life," I commented.

"Yes, I guess so. It didn't seem like that at the time. It was all rather grungy. For one thing, there was very little money. But the marriage did work for a while. Walt was a load of laughs, you know. A real character even then but not as perverse as now. He was great to have around, full of surprises. It fell apart finally, the marriage I mean. But they are still friends, sort of. No hard feelings."

"Yes, I know," I said.

"You know? How?" Betty was surprised. She didn't appear to have heard of my meeting with Lauker. I'd expected the word about my visit to have spread to Betty by now. Maybe she wasn't on that grapevine. That was an interesting possibility.

I told her about it, selectively.

"Oh," was all she said, obviously weighing the implications of the little episode.

"So how do you see it at the moment?" she asked.

"I think it'll now be possible to determine whether Walt is the 'phantom caller' or not. And that would be a start," I answered.

"How? Why?"

"Well, I called his hand. Now he has to re-establish his credibility. How will he choose to do it? What would be in character? You know him, give us a guess."

"I don't know. Something spectacular, I'd say."

"Possibly."

"How would that help?"

"Look. The situation has changed. It's not just in the family, as it were, any more. Hiring me has changed that. It's serious. If it's Walt who is doing the harassment then he has to piss or get off the pot. Which way will he go? That's what I want to know."

"You mean he must either stop or go a lot further?"

"Yes."

"I don't know. I really don't. Walt is capable of anything, I mean either way."

"You believe he is sane enough not to push his luck and stop? That would mean defeat, you know, at least to him."

"When you put it that way, I guess he wouldn't be likely to admit defeat without trying something else first."

"Right. My opinion exactly. My guess is, he will give it one more try. At least that. And what that will be is the big unknown. OK. Let's move on. Tell me, is Lew Davies in it with him? Is he the inside man? What d'you think?"

"Lew! No way. I don't believe it. He's absolutely devoted to Sonia."

"Yeah, yeah. It's what I keep hearing about you all. But isn't Lew the contact between Sonia and Walt? Puts him in the perfect position. Lew keeps Walt informed of what's happening around Sonia. Changes in phone numbers and things like that.

He certainly must have told Walt that I was on the scene. Walt had no trouble putting two and two together when he saw me."

"That could be, of course. But it doesn't mean that Lew is 'in it' with him. Walt could be using him," Betty said with no conviction in her voice. If nothing else, this made Lew into a dummy. Which he wasn't.

"You like Lew, don't you?" I asked.

"Well, for a long time there were the four of us; Sonia, Walt, Lew and me. Then Sonia and Walt split up so there were the three of us. Like I've said, Sonia, Lew and I are close. We go back a long way. Those things matter, you know."

"And now three more have been added, Sedgwick, Bono and Weller."

"Yes. Let's not go into that again," Betty laughed. "I think you know enough about how I feel about them."

Our conversation had done her good. She was smiling, her fair hair shining in the sunlight as we left the restaurant. I declined a lift. I had things to do. She waved cheerfully and drove away.

I felt pretty good about our conversation, too. Betty's performance had been faultless. Consistently, the faithful friend. Only dimly aware of her real feeling for Sonia. Carefully fair to the cast-off husband. Protective of the old friend. Resentful of the influx of heavy-duty lawyers and manager who had destroyed the old threesome and supplanted her, if only partly, in Sonia's life and affection. If it was a part, she'd played it very well.

10

KARL DEERFIELD WAS IN the hotel lobby when I arrived. Sonia wasn't in yet. He introduced himself cautiously, his eyes full of suspicion. Sonia's uncle was a trim, middle-aged man of vaguely military bearing. He spoke in a well modulated tenor, sounding as if constantly listening to his own voice.

"Ha. Good afternoon, good afternoon. I'm Deerfield, Karl Deerfield. Sonia's maternal uncle. Yes, maternal. Surprising that is to some people. Her mother was my sister. Poor Verna. Such a hard life. But don't let me ramble on. How are you, how are you?"

"Fine, thanks. Why is it surprising that you're Sonia's uncle?"

"Maternal uncle, maternal. Because of the names, of course. Sonia uses her mother's name, you see. Always needs to be explained otherwise people think she is illegitimate or something. Won't do, won't do. Dear me, Verna and George were married. Yes, indeed. I was there so I know. But since we both have the same name people take me for her father's brother. So you see I've to make it clear to everyone that I'm her maternal uncle." In addition to being Sonia's maternal uncle Karl Deerfield was an old bore. He could drive any sane person bananas. Having to put up with bores, at least temporarily, is a hazard of my job.

"Yeah," I said, trying to discourage further familial revelations. "Come on up to the apartment. Sonia should be along pretty soon. Meanwhile I would like to get your opinion on all this trouble she's been having. We can talk up there."

"Thank you but no. I just dropped in for a moment. And to meet you. I'm concerned. Naturally, Sonia—and her sister, of course—are my only living relatives. I've neither chick nor child, as they say. Married three times but no children. But you aren't interested in my personal tragedies. Yes, I offered to move in, make a home for Sonia. When all this unpleasantness started. But she prefers a professional. Quite understandable, quite. Family obligations are too restricting for this generation. But I'm always available, always. Should anything happen or if you need me for anything, please just give me a call. My number is—"

"Thanks, I have it. Certainly I'll be in touch if there is anything. Sure you won't come up with me?"

"Well, since you insist. I don't like to push myself, you see." He kept on this type of chatter as we got onto the elevator. I pushed button six. "Perhaps a cup of tea. That would be nice. But young people don't keep up those old country habits. Ah, here we are."

He carried on as I opened the door to the suite, watched me check the place over, order a pot of tea from room service. His eyes were as busy as his mouth.

"Very nice, very nice indeed. We can be all cozy until Sonia arrives. Tell me about yourself. Private detective, a strange job for a young lady. Yes, but I can see it suits you. My, yes. Very efficient. Very. I'm sure Sonia's in good hands." His words were cloying while his voice set up a screen between us. A lonely man's habit or a protective maneuver? Both, probably. Either way it had the desired effect. He didn't have to answer questions because none could be asked. A two-way conversation was impossible.

The tea came. I had a cup to keep him company, and let him talk on. I'd given up trying to break up his monologue. He asked questions about me, about Sonia, about the others and answered them all himself. On and on. I relaxed. Nothing was expected of me. The house phone rang. It was Chester reporting that Sonia and Lew were on their way up from the lobby. I told Karl and he immediately turned into a shrinking violet.

"Oh, dear. I hope Sonia doesn't take it amiss that I dropped in. Just family concern on my part, you know. That's all. Doubtless very tedious but natural, don't you think? Ah, here they are!" as Sonia entered the room, followed by Lew Davies. "How are you, my dear? Well, I trust. And Lew, how are things? Everything still under control. Well, I must fly now, I must.

Overstayed my visit. Very pleasant to have met you, Miss Keremos." —this last in my direction on his way to the door. He fled, without giving me much opportunity to watch the interaction between him and Sonia.

What did happen was interesting enough. Sonia stood there, and without one word, watched him go.

"Bye now, Karl. Everything is A-OK," Lew said, grinning. An unlikely expression on his lips but probably holding some significance for the older man. As the door closed behind Karl Deerfield, Lew turned to me: "Now you've met everybody. Everybody who matters in Sonia's life. What d'you think of us all?"

Before I could make any response to this Sonia broke in. Her voice was imperious, thick with anger and tension.

"Never mind all that crap. I'm tired. Thanks for taking me home, Lew." It was a dismissal. Lew took it well, he winked at me, and said, "OK baby. Get lots of rest. Big day tomorrow. You're going to slay them. Good night." He left, closing the door firmly behind him. Sonia and I were alone among the impersonal hotel furniture.

11

"WHY?" SONIA SAID. "Why did you follow Lew to Walt's place last night? Why didn't you at least discuss it with me first? Isn't your job to protect me, not leave me alone half the night?"

"You hired me to investigate, so, I was investigating. And it helps if the client comes clean. Let me ask you. How come you didn't tell me about Walt? Sending Lew with a cheque for Walt in the middle of the night! I ask you! Tell me why."

"It's nothing to do with anything. No business of yours. I pay Walt, sure. Why not? I can afford it. And he selects the time and place. It's a game we play between us." There wasn't a trace of the vulnerable beauty-in-distress of the day before. Sonia turned her back on me, walked over to the bar and poured herself a drink. She stood for a minute sipping it. The silence was deafening. Finally I said:

"All right. What did Walt tell you about our little chat last night? Was he angry? Annoyed, amused, frightened?"

"I don't know, directly. Lew told me about it. Walt called him last night right after you left. Neither wanted to call me direct so Lew waited until we were together to fill me in. That's how I knew you'd been bothering Walt." Her anger abated. Her words came slowly. I pressed on.

"You feel cut off, don't you? No wonder."

"Yes, yes. I've a million dollars in the bank and I'm more dependent than ever! It doesn't make sense."

"Oh, but it does—"

"Yes, I know. You've made your point. I hired you to help me break out of this dependence. You're an outsider and I'm your client. That means you work for me and only me. And I want to know what you're doing and what's going on around me. I can't bear any more things happening behind my back. Understood?" She was the boss giving orders, not so much angry now as serious and in charge. That was good to see but we had a long way to go yet.

"Sure. You don't really trust any one of them. Not Walt, or Lew or even Betty. Now you are afraid to trust me because I know things you don't know or want me to know. Yesterday you asked for my sympathy; what are you asking from me today? Would it help you if I were deaf, blind and stupid?"

"I didn't say that. Oh, hell! You know what I mean. At least help me understand what's going on. Dead of night trips to Walt don't help in that."

I wasn't so sure but this was no time for fine points. She had to be persuaded to trust me or fire me.

"Let's quit wasting time. Look here, Sonia. I'm not your therapist or your lover, mother or best friend. I don't help people lead their lives, find happiness or clear their acne. I do a specific job in a certain way. Either let me do that job or I'll walk. Make up your mind."

Sonia had finished her drink and was watching me carefully. Then she looked away and nodded to herself. It was a very fetching performance and probably quite genuine.

"Yes. All right, my instincts are still pretty good. They are all I have to go by in any case. Go, do your job. But what do you believe this job is?"

"Primarily to find out who's been threatening you and put a stop to it. That's how those three high-priced employees of yours—Sedgwick and company—briefed me. And as you, yourself told me yesterday." Sonia laughed. Atmosphere began to clear.

"Employees! I like that. They never let me think of them as mere employees. I wonder, does anyone ever think of Arthur that way? It's always more like wise parents looking after a precocious, sensitive child."

"Yeah. It figures. But that's all bull and you know it. So snap out of it. They couldn't get away with treating you like a child unless you let them. You must want it this way somehow. Letting them run your life—"

"Ah, I don't always. Sometimes I play tricks on them." She giggled at the memory. "I do things they don't like and don't expect me to do. Or I don't tell them stuff. They hate that."

"Like maybe depositing your million dollar win in a trust company chequing account where they can't get at it? So they don't even know what you're doing with the loot?" I took a guess.

"Yes, just like that. It's my money, isn't it? Anyway how did you find out about this?"

"Walt told me. Of course it's your money, you needn't be so defensive about it. You can do what you want with it. So why worry what Sedgwick and his ilk say?"

"Oh, stop preaching at me! You, yourself just said it's not your job to help me run my life. Just do your job."

"Happy to oblige. Now that we've determined that it's your money to dispose of as you will, would you be willing to pay off this phantom caller of yours?"

"What! Give this jerk any of my money? Arthur would have a stroke!"

"Arthur's health doesn't interest me. Anyway, I don't mean all the money. Just enough to tempt whoever it is. Well?"

"I guess so. It's just—you are right. I'm afraid of what Arthur would say. He and Ben were dead against paying off extortionists. Isn't that considered bad tactics? Encouraging them?"

"Rules, dumb rules. Forget them. Forget Arthur. I have to have cards to play with. Dollars are aces. Either go along with what I suggest or get yourself another girl."

"I don't know. It could be Walter after all. I just don't know what's best. I think I'd rather wait it out. I wish you would just stick around. I don't like the idea of you going off somewhere doing god knows what and leaving me alone."

"I had to see Walter, you must see that. You hadn't been very honest with me, about Walter and your arrangements with him. Tell me about him."

"Oh, he likes drama. Likes to be the centre of it. I go along with it. Why not? I guess I still have a weak spot for him. He's hard to hate or even dislike."

"That's a matter of opinion. Try me. But that's not the point now. How about that cheque for $500? What's it for? Did he ask for it?"

"No. That junk business of his is not exactly a gold mine, so I help him out. Before my win I gave him $200 a month and bits and pieces whenever I could spare a buck. Arthur kept bugging me about it. Said I couldn't afford the luxury of a leech for an ex-husband. But now I can, so I make it $500 regular. Walter never asked me for anything. It's my idea entirely."

"Five hundred dollars is not very much especially from a millionaire. Maybe he resents it more than he appreciates it."

"He never asked me for any more and he knows I would give him anything he needed. Walt doesn't care about money, per se. That's one reason I like him and why I find it hard to believe he's the extortionist."

"All the others would like it to be Walter."

"I don't blame them. He's done some pretty outrageous things in his time. So it does seem in character. But only on the surface."

"If not Walt, then who?"

"Anyone, no one. I can't really see anyone I know in that role. Perhaps one of the hotel employees. They probably know all about my life, every move. They have the access."

"Could be, but it's a very long shot. Still, I'll check out the most likely ones. I'm more interested in your nearest and dearest. The bevy of Lew, Betty, Ben, Karl, Arthur and Chuck. By the way, did you know that Chuck Weller is a disbarred lawyer?"

"Oh, don't start that. I hoped you wouldn't fall for the obvious. So he's been disbarred, so what? He didn't please the almighty Upper Canada Law Society or something. He's just not part of the establishment, that's all. Doesn't make him a criminal. Chuck's OK. He's been good to me."

"There you go again. 'He's been good to me.' You've been even better to him. And as for 'establishment', well, Arthur Sedgwick isn't exactly an outsider, is he. And he and Weller are as tight as ticks. Which proves nothing in itself but bears watching. You've been around long enough not to be so naive."

"Don't you trust anyone? Must be awful to be like that. I would rather believe the best of people."

"Nuts. Believing the best of everyone is not very different from believing the worst of everyone. I know whom I can trust. You've never had the guts to find out who is to be trusted and who isn't. So now you can't trust anyone. Now here is your moment of truth. Will you trust me and go along with me, a stranger? Will you follow my suggestions or not? Let's have a decision. You and I have fiddle-farted around long enough."

There was a long moment of silence. We'd been going at each other hammer and tongs for what seemed like hours. Sonia had damn few options. Go along with me or be alone again. She said:

"All right. Damn Arthur anyway. You make a lot more sense. I'll offer a pay-off next time this bastard calls. You'll have to coach me on what to say and how much to offer. But it can't be tomorrow. I'll be out all day. We're doing a demo tape with the new group. Lew and I have been working at it for weeks. We're due in the studio at 8:30 a.m. It'll be a long, hard grind. Everyone will be there some time during the day. D'you plan to come too?"

"Since everyone else will be there then I'd better, eh? I'll take you to the studio and check it out. Then we'll see. But let's leave it for now. We've both had about enough for tonight."

"OK. How about a nightcap? What will you have?"

It had been a heavy, exhausting conversation. I felt Sonia's tension and responded to it. She was the most exciting woman I'd met in months. I wished that I had the energy to make love to her. But sleep was what I needed. The previous night had been short on sack time. I'd one drink with her and went to my room leaving her huddled in front of the TV.

I sat on my bed and considered Sonia and Walter. Their relationship was somewhat unusual, but then they weren't your average ex-couple. Was that story of the $500 believable? I was uncomfortable with the amount more than anything. Hard to ignore, yet not enough to do anyone any good. Maybe it was irrelevant, just as Sonia claimed. The kind of item which tends to sidetrack an investigation. On the other hand, it was money out of the relevant account. Next, in whose interest was the war of nerves against Sonia? For that's all that it amounted to, so far. Walt had suggested Chuck Weller, a good possibility. But in combination with Betty Grelick? Not likely. I couldn't see Betty in combination with anyone but Lew Davies.

My mind slipped on to Karl Deerfield. Certainly Sonia didn't reciprocate any of that family feeling he kept plugging. So what? Families are strange things.

Next I considered the Arthur Sedgwick, Ben Bono and Chuck Weller triumvirate. They appeared to be running Sonia Deerfield and to own her lock, stock and barrel yet none of them had direct access to her million. An angle worth pursuing. A million dollars in a chequing account! Quite a temptation.

Taking them one at a time. Ben Bono. His pursuit of Sonia pre-dated her win. But money is no impediment to love. Would he try to scare her into marrying him for protection?

Arthur Sedgwick was the hardest to figure and the most interesting. What did he want? He already had money. But can a guy like that ever have enough?

Chuck Weller again. It was safe to assume that he needed money more than most. With some outside accomplice to make the calls and harass Sonia, Weller could hope to shake her down at one remove and remain safe. That was the simplest explanation. But would he wait this long to make his move, to present specific demands? Hardly. A fast pay-off was more in character and fitted his circumstances better.

I'm not what you might call a cerebral type of investigator. Action is more my strong point. Speculation of this kind is OK; it helps to clarify matters but seldom leads to any concrete results. What the case needed was a little more direct action. I fell asleep planning to stir the pot and see what happened. As it turned out, someone was way ahead of me.

12

NEXT MORNING LEW DAVIES arrived unexpectedly as Sonia and I were having breakfast. This time instead of castoffs he wore expensive chinos, a pressed shirt and the fanciest white leather joggers I've ever seen. It was seven-thirty and here he was as full of smiles 'n' chuckles as a box of bonbons, spreading the Welsh equivalent of blarney far and wide.

"Good morning to you, good morning, ladies. A fine day, I know we're going to have a great session, Sonia. In my bones, I know it. The boys and girls are all ready and just a-raring to go. A great session, I can feel it. We'll kill them dead, I promise."

He was totally hyper, went on and on, wouldn't sit down, almost spilled a cup of coffee and got on my nerves. What a way to start the day! Sonia must have been used to this, she took it calmly, and eventually managed to settle Lew down by pretending to listen while he talked shop a mile a minute. Over my second cup of coffee I was faced with listening to a long and involved discussion on the problems between Terry Armour, the bass player and Wayne Kilynski, the drummer. The ins and outs of their private lives and those of everyone else in the group. Or the Herd. 'Sonia Deerfield and the Herd,' that was the billing. I got up, suggested Lew drive Sonia to the studio as I had some errands to run and would join them later. Anything to get away from this drivel. Lew was delighted at the suggestion, gave me detailed and confusing instructions on how to get to the studio. Sonia looked understanding, amused and gorgeous.

Of course I didn't do any errands. My job was to check out the recording studio and be there when Sonia arrived. So I took myself and my spanking new 4X4 on a spin along the lakefront to the Lakeshore Boulevard location of Tri-Met Studios. It was housed, as I expected, in a heavily refurbished warehouse building, behind a tall wire fence. A bored, middle-aged security man checked me in and directed me to the back door entrance from the parking lot. He was happy to talk.

"Save you going all the way around to the front door. Just park in one of them spaces what don't have a name or number on them and you'll be OK. Hey, how many cars comin' in today, any idea?" I said I didn't know how many but mentioned a white Volvo which would be there soon.

"White Volvo. That's the star, eh. In a Volvo. Not what I would drive if I had their money. Never can figure out these recording folks. Rock and roll, eh. D'you know we once had a guy arrive here in a hearse? Silly I call it. How d'you like your truck? It's new, right?"

I told him I liked it fine. We went on chatting and I got quite a lot of information out of him in the process. Like when he went off duty and how hard it was for unauthorized people to get into the building.

"We aren't really here to stop anyone if they want to go in, see. All they need to say is that they've business at Tri-Met, that's all. But it keeps the parking lot from being filled-up by local people, people who have no business here at all. And like, there is expensive equipment in that building and performers bring their instruments and all. So we protect the place like. Never had no burglary yet but things do disappear all the time. Just disappear. Can't do nothing about that, not really. But it's a good job s'long as you don't mind spending your day on your feet, and alone mostly. I get an hour off for lunch and fifteen minutes break at ten and at three. Joseph, the caretaker like, a coloured guy, is supposed to come out and spell me, but as often as not I don't see him. They keep him real busy inside, I guess. But it doesn't matter, I have my lunch here, the coffee wagon stops right in front. I quit at six, evening shift comes on. They lock up at ten most evenings and get to sleep the rest of their shift. Except when there's someone working in there all night. Then one night man has to be awake to let them in and out through the back door and this gate. The front doors close at five-thirty when the office closes. After that everyone has to use the back door and come out past us here at the gate, see? That's how it is around here. You in security work too, eh? Women in everything nowadays. You look more like you could look after yourself all right. D'you like the work?" I said, yes I did, and thanked him for letting me in on the set-up at Tri-Met. Professional courtesy is very important in our business, I said. He agreed gravely and waved me on.

I drove around the parking lot once just to get familiarized, then I parked where he'd indicated, not far from the back door. There were only a few cars in as yet—time was eight-ten a.m.—but a number of sound trucks, including a large CBC mobile unit,were parked up against the wall next to the building itself. The Canadian Broadcasting Corporation is very short of studio space in Toronto and probably had rented space at Tri-Met.

I walked through the wide, heavy, sound-proof door. On my right a passage led to what I took to be front office country—executive offices, client reception, viewing rooms, administration and such like. Panelled walls, floors covered with flashy wall-to-wall. On the left the passage took a turn and led me past washrooms, past equipment rooms and storage to a series of sound studio doors. I entered one at random. It was empty. In the next one I was greeted by the raised eyebrows of a young technician.

"You from the Universal Sound outfit?" she asked.

I mumbled something about Sonia Deerfield.

"That's it. Universal booked in. Nobody here yet but me. The boys should be here momentarily. There's coffee in the green room. And you can go sit in the booth and wait for your party."

She was friendly and more obliging towards the uninitiated than in my experience is usual with technicians. As it turned out, once her buddies arrived, all male, she cut me dead just like the rest.

Instead of making for the glass booth which hung like an allseeing eye over the studio floor, I wandered through all available doors, checked the green room—real, fresh coffee—

the location of the drinking fountain, telephones including extensions, locked closets. Satisfied that I had the layout of the place memorized, I finally made my way up the steps to the glass-fronted control booth of Studio B. No sooner had I sat down than Chuck Weller appeared. We dispensed with preliminaries.

"Fascinating, isn't it?" he said with more animation than he had shown in Arthur Sedgwick's office. He moved his chin to indicate the studio around us. "A whole world. All over my head, of course. But fascinating. Don't you agree?"

"Yeah, fascinating. What's your part in all this? Since you're Sonia's manager don't you have to know all about this recording business?"

"No, no. Sonia and Lew between them make all the creative decisions. I'm the business manager, you know. My job is to sell Sonia and whatever package she and Lew come up with. Contracts especially. And generally publicity, promotion— Betty's very helpful in that, she really knows the ropes—and take care of all business details so Sonia doesn't have to bother about any of it."

"You pay all her bills, do you?" I asked.

"Yes, indeed. In consultation with Ben Bono and the accountant we look after all her interests. Yes, indeed. It's getting to be quite a substantial business, you know."

"Oh, yeah? Then I guess you know who all is on Sonia's payroll, right?"

"Naturally."

"How about Betty Grelick. You just mentioned her. Is she on the payroll? How much?" I pushed some more, almost at random.

"Not regularly, no. But we do use her professional services once in a while, as I've said. As a consultant. She sends us a bill for her time. That's all."

"And how about Walter Lauker? And Karl Deerfield? Sonia supports them, doesn't she?"

Weller stopped looking into space over my shoulder and

actually looked me in the eye for a few seconds. He wasn't happy with the topic of conversation.

"Well now, no. I couldn't say. Not from the company account, no. Are you sure she still pays Lauker? I thought Arthur said—" He ran down, afraid he'd said too much.

"So you don't in fact look after all her interests, do you? She must have quite a healthy personal account which you guys don't control. Don't even get to see who gets what from it."

"Of course, of course. But that's small potatoes, that personal stuff. We, that is Ben Bono and I, we control her business, her assets, manage her career, you know. That's what matters."

"Really. Funny. Why are you trying to make me believe that you have your hands on her million dollars? My information is that Sonia picked up her win and immediately socked it away in a trust company account in her personal name. So only she has access to all that cash. Care to comment?"

"Comment? No. No, I have nothing to say. Except that I fail to see what business this is of yours. It isn't pertinent to the job you've been hired for."

I grinned at him.

"Come on, Mr. Weller. Both of us know it's damn pertinent. However, I expect you will want to consult your boss, I mean Mr. Arthur B. Sedgwick, not Sonia, before we can get any further in this little charade."

Weller brushed ash off his shabby suit, got up and left without another word.

"There's a telephone with lots of privacy just down the hall on your right," I shouted after him but he didn't acknowledge my helpfulness.

I felt good at having stirred up something; Chuck was certainly on his way to call Arthur for instructions. I relaxed and watched the goings-on on the studio floor. During my conversation with Chuck Weller members of the Herd had started to arrive tugging at their instruments. Two or three house technicians materialized. There was an uncoordinated bustle as young/old and old/young men went about their business with no apparent reference to anyone else. Instruments were tuned; microphones moved about, switched off and on, tested; cables rattled; switches flicked; knobs turned. It looked random but was in fact purposeful.

It was close to nine before Sonia and Lew made their appearance, accompanied by an important looking man in a snow white suit. He and Lew went directly into the control booth while Sonia circled the studio floor kissing and hugging everyone in the Herd, especially her vocal back-up, a trio of women who had arrived together just before her. Then she joined Lew and Snow White in the booth. On the studio floor the atmosphere subtly changed, while the three principals in the booth ignored not only my presence but everything else. Clearly all this was ritual. For a good ten minutes both the group on the floor of the studio and the three people in the booth gossiped away. I could hear Sonia and the two men with her discussing various arcane matters such as the tastes of record company A&R men, with reference to the pieces they were about to record. Then the conversation turned to conducting the recording session. This had been agreed upon before but now had to be restated for the record. In the fullness of time agreement was reached and the ritual could be concluded. Lew and the white-clad man, whose name was Lennie, in turn kissed and hugged Sonia for luck, presumably. She gave me only a slow grin and left the booth for the studio floor. Lew Davies turned to me briefly. Here, on his own ground he appeared quite different from the ditherer of early morning. Gone was the nervous ingratiating bull-shitter and in his place was the Man-in-Charge.

"Helen, we'll be at it now without a break for perhaps three hours. So feel free to leave, the green room is at your disposal. There's coffee and food laid on. Chuck is here already, I see. Arthur and Ben will probably drop in later. See you at lunch. That's it. OK Lennie, let's get to work."

Lennie sat down in front of an enormous 48-channel board, Lew Davies standing beside him, studio mike in hand. Suddenly the regular lights went out and the booth was bathed in black light. The mighty console glowed with vivid Day-Glo. The effect was—what can I say—weird? dramatic? stunning? childish? All of that. I left the booth, grinning. Expensive toys are strangely fascinating. I'm old enough to recall when music flourished without benefit of electronic gizmos, computers or, for that matter bizarre light effects. Now it takes a zillion dollars in electronic gadgets to cut a simple record and then it needs another zillion for a hyped-up video to make the Top 40 where the pay-off is. Big, big money. There is no way for anyone to make it on talent alone. In fact talent is just about irrelevant. Sonia was good, damn good, but without the heavy-duty orchestration, without the electronics, without the hype and scores of people and the $$$ behind her she had no chance of making it. The quality of her voice—like hot, dark, bitter-sweet chocolate—her distinctive style, her subtle phrasing, years of experience, all that would amount to very little unless and until processed by the monster music industry. Made into a saleable product. But that's just my opinion and nobody was paying me for it.

The next few hours passed uneventfully. Chuck Weller sat in the green room reading and re-reading the *Globe & Mail*, hardly acknowledging my existence. I wandered around, spent time with the receptionist at the front desk, said hello to the busy caretaker, asked questions of various free-floating technicians. Eventually I came to the attention of an officious young executive who inquired who I was and what I was doing. I told him politely that I was with Sonia Deerfield and Universal Sound. He immediately turned deferential.

"Great thing for Miss Deerfield to have Universal show so much interest. Guess they must be pretty sure it's going to fly. Pretty sure they will like the demo tape here and especially in New York, I mean. Looks like a contract is in the bag, eh. Of course you can never be certain, can you? This is a funny business, don't you think?" He was fishing.

"Funny? How?"

"Well, for one thing you never know about record companies. One day you're a hero with them, next you're a bum.

I've been in this business long enough, even worked for a record company, Capstain Records, for a while myself before coming to Tri-Met, but I still never try to second guess them. I was sort of surprised Universal put so much up front into Sonia. Oh, don't misunderstand me, I know she's good and should sell, properly promoted. But with the market the way it is these days, all these corporate take-overs, the uncertainty in the trade, it's unusual for a relatively unknown pop singer to get so much attention at this stage from a major company like Universal. Don't you agree?"

He really was interested in what was going on but I couldn't help him. I said something noncommittal and edged away. It was good to have my suspicions about the Universal deal confirmed but I still didn't know what it all meant. I was impatient to get to Arthur Sedgwick. It figured that he would appear shortly. Then we would see.

Indeed at about eleven forty-five Arthur Sedgwick arrived, closely followed by Ben Bono. Both men went into the sound booth, exchanged pleasantries with an impatient Lew Davies, waved at Sonia and the Herd. While Ben prepared to watch and listen to further proceedings, Arthur excused himself and went to talk to Chuck Weller. All I got was a stately nod. Somewhat ostentatiously I made my way to the front desk and took up my conversation with the highly decorative receptionist. I didn't freak her out, an effect I sometimes have on women in her job. On the contrary, she seemed quite taken with my company, so time passed pleasantly. True, only part of my mind was on her and on our talk. I expected Arthur Sedgwick to approach me at any moment. He did.

13

"AH, THERE YOU ARE, Helen. Good day to you. Forgive me interrupting, Miss Callenby," Sedgwick intoned, with a glance at the name plate on the reception desk. "I would like to take Miss Keremos away for a while. Do excuse us." Unlike many less imposing men, Arthur Sedgwick was unfailingly courteous to his 'inferiors'. Phyllis Callenby was charmed; Arthur Sedgwick had made her day. Which didn't say much for the men she was ordinarily exposed to if compared to them he was such a gem.

I made the right noises at Sedgwick and we walked away together towards the back of the building.

"Sonia and Lew are having lunch sent in for themselves and the band." He continued, "They don't want to interrupt the session any more than necessary. I understand it's going very well. So I thought perhaps you and I could step out for a short lunch and talk. There is a rather good Japanese restaurant not too far. Would a sushi bar lunch suit you?"

"That would be just fine. Are Mr. Bono and Mr. Weller going to join us?" I asked, all innocence.

"No. No. I believe they have some business matters to discuss. Very tedious that would be for you. I had in mind a tête-à-tête; just you and me." From anyone else that would have sounded coy, not from Sedgwick. Again I made the right noises. A stylish Mercedes waited outside. Sedgwick drove, filling the space between us with polite chitchat.

There was no room at the bar but we managed to procure a secluded table and sat down. Sedgwick handled the situation with consummate skill. All the subtle, and not so subtle, details of getting in and out of the car, going through doors, deciding on a table, ordering drinks. These can be problematic nowadays when women and men get together. There is a fine and important line between sexist oversolicitude and an ostentatious boorishness on the part of the male to emphasize a spurious 'equality'. In this respect Sedgwick's manner was impressively secure. We went through the social niceties with no sweat at all. I ordered a carafe of sake and prepared to enjoy myself. I was being carefully softened up by an expert. It's not paranoia to consider every move of a man like Sedgwick as part of a power play. By life-long practice, certainly by training and probably by native inclination, people like Sedgwick view every situation in adversarial terms. Every relationship, every moment of their lives they see as win or lose situations. Conquer or be conquered. Life is a series of those sorts of choices.

We were almost through the delicate soup when he made the first move in the battle.

"I have to confess, Helen, that I misjudged you. I'd no idea that you would be so eager to interest yourself in my affairs." More in sorrow than in anger.

"I don't interest myself in your affairs, Arthur, only in my client's affairs."

"Come now, don't pretend to be obtuse. You were not hired to investigate the business arrangements between Miss Deerfield and myself. Only to protect her from harassment and, if possible, find the culprit."

"There are a number of answers to that, all of them good. Let's try this one first: the caller wants a piece of Sonia's million. It's elementary to find out who already has access to that million. You don't."

"Does that make me suspect in some way? No, that answer won't do. The thing which upset Chuck and which disturbs me now is not that you know in which bank account that money is deposited at present. Not at all. That's a matter of record and no secret. What bothers me is that you presume to draw conclusions on the basis of this minor point, you view it in a suspicious light. Now, that concerns me."

"Why? Why should it concern you? I am paid to be suspicious of everyone. Aren't you stretching credibility a bit to insist that access to a million dollars is a 'minor point'? Would you be asking me, or anyone, to believe that you are totally above temptation? And how about Chuck Weller? Is he also above suspicion?"

"I see. You believe that Weller and I are after Sonia's million. But she only won it recently. So what were we after before she had the money?"

"I don't necessarily 'believe' anything. But you and Chuck Weller are up to something. It's pointless to claim that the million is irrelevant. I was clearly given to understand that the three of you—Weller, Bono and you—administered Sonia's whole business, including that million. It isn't true. Why did you lie? Now you are calling it a minor point, which is absurd. Why?"

"Come now, Helen. If any of us were after Sonia's money the very last thing we would do is this harassment campaign. It's not in our interest no matter how you construe it."

"Agreed. Nobody said that the phantom caller is part of your scheme. Quite the reverse, it must be an infernal nuisance, a diversion, and disturbance. You hoped the trouble would soon die down, that's why you did nothing about it for so long. Too long. But it didn't go away, in fact it got bigger and potentially more dangerous. You couldn't afford not to do anything about it. So finally you agreed to hire someone to look into the problem. I bet you had some tame dick all ready to take the case. But Sonia put her foot down, she insisted on getting me. And you had no way of overruling her, especially since she could pay me directly from her personal pocket, without going through the business account which you control. You didn't like that possibility. How am I doing so far?"

"I suppose it could look like that to an outsider. But it's all based on a misapprehension."

"What misapprehension? Give me a hint."

"Please Helen, the situation does not call for facetiousness. You know very well that what I'm questioning is your assumption, now explicitly expressed, that I, and Bono and Weller, have some ulterior motives contrary to Sonia's best interests. That is not the case."

"That depends on how and by whom her best interests are defined. I intend to have her define them for me rather than leave it to you or the lovesick Mr. Bono or that pillar of the Ontario bar, Mr. Charles Weller."

I bit into a slice of luscious sashimi and wondered how long it would take for Sedgwick to drop all this sweet reasonableness.

"I see. You've found out about Chuck's misfortune. That's too bad. You can't be so naive as to assume that disbarment automatically makes him a villain," Sedgwick said, still in the pleasant mode.

"No, but it bothers me that Sonia was allowed to believe that he was disbarred for some anti-establishment misdemeanour. You and I both know that realistically speaking there is only one reason for which lawyers are ever disbarred. And that is blatant fraud, misappropriation of client funds too obvious to be swept under the rug. Weller didn't lose his licence to practise law in this province for being too radical or even for being a lousy lawyer. He was kicked out because he stole and got caught. Period. Sonia should've been told. Why wasn't she?"

"It wasn't deemed necessary. I can assure you that Chuck wouldn't take a cent from Sonia to which he's not entitled."

"And you can totally guarantee that. Sure, I believe you. He's in your pocket. But that's still not the point. You guarantee this and that; you decide what Sonia should be told; you define her interests. Not good enough."

"My dear Helen, I assure you Ben Bono has a full say in everything we decide about Sonia's career. You yourself called him 'lovesick'. Yes, he's very much in love with Sonia. Surely you can see that he only has her happiness at heart? You can't believe that he would be party to any plot, by Chuck or me, which would harm Sonia in any way! The idea is ludicrous!"

"Ben Bono's self-interest regarding Sonia Deerfield makes him the last person whose judgment I would trust. All three of you may have the best intentions towards her but they are your intentions. You don't even tell her everything yet you want to make her accept your judgment as her own. That I'll never buy."

"I see. Well, that's that. I tried. I'm afraid I'll have to recommend to Sonia that you be dismissed from the case. Too bad. No reflection on your honesty or professional capacity. However, it's clear that you take too much upon yourself, that you don't follow instructions. That won't do. Your fee will be paid, of course, and you needn't worry about references. I'll be more than pleased to testify to your diligence and loyalty." Sedgwick had finally decided to play hardball. I laughed.

"Big of you, Arthur. Let's see what Sonia has to say before you overwhelm me with your generosity. I wouldn't count on getting rid of me quite that easily."

"Are you implying that Sonia will not go along with my recommendation? And that of Bono and Weller, her manager? Do you really expect that she'll keep you on against our advice? I don't believe that you could've gotten that much influence on her in such a short period. Why, she only met you yesterday!"

"All I did was point out that your definition of her 'best interests' needn't necessarily square with hers. You have your own axes to grind. It doesn't take a hell of a lot of 'influence' to get that across. She really knew it all along and it just needed an outsider to put it into words. Whatever happens about me, I think you are going to find it much harder now to sustain your role as an authority figure with Sonia. Brace yourself, she's begun to think about you, and the others, as employees! Tough."

There wasn't much left to say after that. Sedgwick paid, I thanked him politely for a nice lunch, we got into the smooth Mercedes and drove back to the studio in silence.

14

BACK AT THE TRI-MET STUDIOS it was old home week. Everyone was there. The first person I saw as we drove into the parking lot was Betty Grelick. She was just opening the back door and walked in without seeing us. I caught up with her in the hall, leaving Sedgwick to his own dark thoughts.

"So, here we are! I hear the session is going great. I thought I would drop by and sit in on it for a while." She appeared pleased to see me and quite untroubled by her problems of the day before. "Lew called me and said that Karl is here. Apparently he arrived after you and Arthur had left and insisted on joining Sonia and Lew for lunch."

"Insisted? You mean he talked so constantly they couldn't get him to understand he wasn't wanted?"

"Something like that, I guess. He can be a very stubborn old man when he wants to." Betty laughed.

"Still, it's rather out of character, isn't it? Yesterday Sonia cut him dead and he left her apartment like a dog with his tail between his legs. So how come today he's pushy?"

"You'll have to ask Lew just what happened. Oh, there he is!"

Indeed Lew Davies appeared from the door to the men's washroom. He looked distracted, if not upset.

"Am I glad the two of you are here! Can you get Karl off Sonia's back? I've never seen him go on like this."

"What set him off?" I asked.

"Walt, I guess. Yes, Lauker is here. It all started to pop after you and Sedgwick went to lunch. People began to arrive, hoping to catch Sonia at our break. She and I and Lennie were going to have a short working lunch and get back to recording as soon as possible when first Walt arrived, then Karl—"

"And then the shit really hit the fan," Betty finished for him.

"Exactly. Karl is convinced that Walter is behind all this trouble. He feels that his place is at Sonia's side all the time. To protect her. He noted that you weren't there, Helen. He made a lot of that in fact; you're supposed to be bodyguarding and not gadding about."

"How is Sonia?" Betty inquired anxiously.

"Upset, what did you think? This just might ruin the rest of the afternoon. Unless we can get rid of Uncle Karl. And Walt also, of course."

"My fault for being away. I'll try and sort all this out. Betty, why don't you take Sonia away somewhere so we can deal with these guys. Go to the washroom, that way Karl and Walt can't follow you there. Lew, you take Walt aside. Introduce him to the Herd, show him the equipment, buy him a lollipop, anything. And let's hope Arthur and his party keep out of the fray."

I had the right idea but it was too late. In the green room Karl Deerfield at his most soldierly was confronting Arthur Sedgwick. The two men faced each other like bantam roosters, apparently oblivious of the rest of us. Sonia sat silently in one corner, looking bored and beautiful. Walt Lauker displayed a set of bad teeth at me in a derisive grin, Chuck Weller and Ben Bono stood uncomfortably behind Sedgwick, for all the world like seconds behind their principal. It was not clear what had started the donnybrook.

"My daddy can lick your daddy," I whispered to Betty as we took in the tableau. She giggled. Lew gave us a disapproving glance. His sense of humour couldn't take the strain.

Karl's voice went on and on.

"Mr. Sedgwick, I'm surprised, yes, surprised. A man of your reputation and standing. Perhaps undeserved. Indeed undeserved—"

Here Sedgwick made the mistake of trying to get a word in.

"What seems to be the trouble, Mr. Deerfield? What's bothering you so much?"

"Bothering me! You have to ask, do you? My dear sir, you confirm my worst fears about your judgment. Yes, judgment. You've betrayed your trust, sir. Yes, betrayed." Again Arthur Sedgwick broke in, exasperated.

"Now, Mr. Deerfield, control yourself, please. I can see you're under strain, otherwise I would hold you responsible for your words. To say of a lawyer that he's betrayed his trust is slander. Be careful what you say. Now what, sir, do you mean?"

"The truth, ah! The truth! You can't face it, can you? You threaten me with the law. Indeed, sir. It's as I thought. As family, as Sonia's only remaining relative (Karl conveniently forgot Sonia's sister), it is my duty to speak up. I had hoped, yes sir, in my innocence I hoped that you Mr. Sedgwick, would take care of our little girl, would see her safe, yes safe. Protected from dangerous criminals like this man she was once misguided enough to marry, this man Lauker. Yet I find him here. And Sonia unguarded, unprotected. You take your responsibilities lightly, indeed, sir. Well, I do not." He was still in full spate when Sonia broke in.

"Shut up, Karl. Nobody asked you here."

He ignored her and continued his oration.

"I know it's hard. Yes, I know. Dear Sonia is her own worst enemy. Just look at the people she surrounds herself with. False friends. Unscrupulous employees. Yes, unscrupulous. It was up to you sir, and you betrayed your trust. This man Lauker threatened her life, sir. And there he is as bold as brass. And this unnatural female you've hired. What are we to make of that? She leaves my poor niece unprotected just as this man Lauker arrives! With your connivance, I understand, Mr. Sedgwick." Karl Deerfield gave me a killing glare, took a fresh breath and proceeded. He was having a ball. For that matter so was I. And Walter Lauker. Nobody else.

"Fire her! Right now I demand that you fire her, this Helen Keremos or whatever heathen name she goes under. Yes, heathen. I'll protect my niece from now on. I demand your full cooperation."

Arthur Sedgwick did as pretty a flip-flop as it has been my privilege to witness. Without a misstep he and Karl Deerfield were suddenly on the same side.

"I'm glad we agree on that, Mr. Deerfield. We can certainly dispense with Miss Keremos. It's obvious that the situation does not require her services. We can deal with it between us as reasonable people. Both she and Mr. Lauker will be asked to leave. I'm sure the whole matter can be settled quite amicably without Miss Keremos's assistance."

Sedgwick's tone and whole demeanour implied that all was now settled. Deerfield's accusations against him were ignored. All would now be peace, love and good vibes. Then Sonia spoke again, this time not letting herself be ignored.

"Just a cotton-picking minute, you two. I'm tired of having you arrange my life for me. Just get out, both of you. Arthur, I'll talk to you later. As for you Karl, go away! I don't want to see you. Helen stays, understand! And Walt can come to see me anytime! Quit running my life! Now beat it, I've work to do."

If it was only an act, it was superb. Her voice was icy. There wasn't a tremor in it. Walt clapped and muttered sotto voce, "Brava! Brava! " The rest stirred uneasily. They weren't used to this Sonia. Arthur went up to her and turned on the authoritative charm.

"Now, my dear. You're under strain. Why don't you go on with the session and let me handle this situation? Really, it's for the best. Let Miss Keremos go, we don't need outsiders. I'll deal with Mr. Lauker and Mr. Deerfield. Of course, he will stay and protect you. After all he's your uncle and only wants what's best for you. And so do I, my dear, so do we all."

"Oh, go away Arthur! Go and take Uncle Karl with you. Just leave me alone. I want Helen to stay, and that's my business."

"All right my dear, as you wish. We'll talk about it all tomorrow at my office."

"Tomorrow, sure, that's great," Sonia said with evident relief. She couldn't sustain her hardnosed stance for very long. Arthur Sedgwick, the old campaigner, smiled, patted her shoulder and beat a tactical retreat. Tomorrow was another day.

Betty went up to Karl Deerfield who was prattling on although no one was listening, took his arm and led him away. He went obediently. I turned to take a good look at Walter Lauker, whose very presence had precipitated this scene. He was still grinning, snapping his fingers and repeating, "Bis, bis, encore" under his breath. For the occasion he was decked out à la English country squire in heavy tweeds and enormous brogues and—an important touch—his socks still didn't match. He gave me a wicked grimace and turned to Lew who was trying to get his attention.

"All right, Lew, I'll go quietly. Thank you for inviting me to this matinee. I wouldn't have missed it for the world. It's such a treat for us mere amateurs to witness a superb professional performance. Experts at work, so to speak. Very encouraging. Shows what can be done with proper training, experience—"

"—and motivation. Don't forget motivation." I couldn't resist getting into the spirit of it all. He produced a deep bow in my direction.

"Of course, of course. Motivation. One must be properly motivated to excel. Don't you agree, Lew?"

But Lew wouldn't join the game. He said impatiently, "Walt, stop playing the fool. Don't encourage him, Helen. Come on out, out, Walter. Amuse yourself elsewhere."

"I think I'll wait until Arthur and dear Uncle Karl have departed. Then I'll steal away."

"All right, just don't steal anything else. I wouldn't put it past you." Lew turned, looking for Sonia. She had left quietly, probably to pull herself together in the women's washroom. Lew gave an exasperated sigh, lit a cigarette and walked out. The room was clearing. Chuck and Ben were gone, following their leader. Only Walter Lauker and I remained.

"What odds that Arthur will prevail tomorrow and get you fired?" he asked. I wouldn't rise to the bait, so he continued, "Arthur and Uncle Karl are right, much as I hate to admit it. You're a bad influence on Sonia, and on the situation generally. It was more fun before you got into the act. Why don't you pick up your marbles, such as they are, and withdraw gracefully? You really have no business here." He was deadly serious.

"Stay in character, Walt," I answered.

15

AFTER ALL THAT NOONTIME EXCITEMENT, the afternoon seemed an anti-climax. Only Sonia, Lew and Chuck remained, attending to business. The rest trucked off, singly or in bunches. Chuck Weller took turns with me in the booth watching and listening to Lew put Sonia and the Herd through a complex repertoire, in the green room drinking coffee and snacking or promenading around the hall and parking lot. We were careful to give each other a wide berth for obvious reasons. I learned a good bit about recording that I hadn't known before and even more about Sonia. All of which was interesting enough but still could not hold my attention for the span of time required. By late afternoon I was bored and so, it appeared, was Chuck.

The assembled company, musicians and crew, drank a tremendous amount of Coke. The addiction was general, and the only one in evidence at the recording session. Things had changed in the recording industry (among others), I thought idly, since the balmy days of fifteen years ago.

When Sonia called it quits, Lew tried to argue, insisting that they were wasting precious studio time, but Sonia cut him off.

"I can afford it. I've had enough. I bet we all have. Let's pack up now, we can be back next week. That "Who are you, Baby?" number is good but needs a lot of work. So let's rehearse it some more and get it right next time." She looked tired and restless.

"OK, OK. You've heard the lady, boys and girls." Lew was the NCO passing on the General's orders to the troops. He continued with instructions, comments and admonitions while Sonia walked off the floor, chatting with, kissing and hugging each member of the Herd as she went. Chuck and I, together for once, met her in the green room where Lew joined us minutes later.

"What a day, what a day! What d'you think, Lew, how d'we do?"

"Great, just great, Chuck! We've some good cuts now on tape, just two or three more numbers and we'll have a record that'll blow their minds. We'll write our own contract with any major label on the continent," Lew enthused. Sonia smiled at us and translated.

"I guess it's good enough to go with. But Lew, you should leave all the hype to Chuck. It's his job. Well, what do you think, Chuck?"

"Universal Sound is in the bag, you know that. Arthur—" Chuck started out to make a speech.

Sonia interrupted.

"Arthur, Arthur! He's got it all arranged in advance, doesn't he! Why do we bother with these sessions and with a demo tape then?"

Chuck looked concerned and jumped in to explain.

"Now you know it's not all fixed. That's not what I meant. We do have to sell it in New York. But with Arthur's influence—" He kept on making the same error. Sonia burst in again.

"Fuck Arthur's influence. Either I'm good enough or I'm not."

Lew intervened.

"Don't be naive, Sonia. Hell, you know better. Having Arthur behind us makes a lot of difference. You know damn well how hard it is to break into the big time without a lot of influence. Everyone here knows you're great, Arthur's just helping to get the big boys on side."

"Oh, I know, I know. Sorry, you guys. Forget I said anything. Just ignore me, I'm tired." Sonia dismissed the subject with a wave of her hand. Her hair shone like a halo around her drawn face. She included me in her glance and suddenly smiled and moved towards me.

"Helen, let's you and I get out of here. Let's just go for a drive then get hammered somewhere. And not talk about the music biz, not once. Would you like that?" Would I like that!

"Great idea. Anything you say. My pleasure. Let's take my new wheels out on the highway." I was dithering like an idiot.

"Hey, you've that neat little truck, don't you? Can I drive

it? Is it hard?" She grabbed my arm, looked into my face as we walked out of the room leaving Lew and Chuck looking at each other uncertainly. They didn't like it but there wasn't much they could do about it.

I'll never forget that short walk across the parking lot. Sonia chattered, holding my hand, an edge of hysteria in her voice.

"A great machine this is, Helen. What a life! How I envy you! You can just travel across the country anytime you feel like it, eh?" I tried very hard to say that no, it wasn't quite that simple, but she wasn't listening. "Just get in and go. Oh, how I would love that! Yes, maybe I'll do it someday, soon."

"No reason why you couldn't, Sonia," I said as we got into the vehicle, Sonia on the driver's and I on the passenger's side. "Here, let me show you the ropes." Sonia, happy as a kid, sat behind the wheel admiring the computerized instrument panel, the 40 channel CB, the phone, the stereo cassette player. She played with the map light, the spotlight and all the other gadgets which I had had installed in the buggy in a moment of weakness. She revved the engine and watched the tachometer light up on the instrument face. To get the hang of the five gears before moving, she double declutched expertly from first into second, then into third—

There was an almighty bang from right under our feet and the truck exploded. I felt myself being thrown against the door which, mercifully not locked, sprang open. I blacked out as I hit the pavement.

The complete blackout lasted only a minute or so, but I remained out of it for all practical purposes throughout the rescue operation. Lying on the ground unable and unwilling to move I watched the police cars, the ambulances as if from an enormous distance. Everything was happening through a fog, in slow motion. I saw Lew Davies' horrified face. I saw Sonia lifted into the ambulance. I felt it happening to me. There was no pain, just numbness.

Pain came on the trip to hospital, strapped to a stretcher. I was grateful for the shot which put me out. I remember nothing more.

16

THE FIRST THING I became conscious of was that I was surrounded. Dozens of people, some in white coats, loomed over little old me, blocking the view. I tried to wave them away. It didn't work.

"She's awake," someone said. I nodded to confirm this. That was a mistake. The discomfort—it wasn't yet pain—woke me up further. I became conscious not only of the room and the people around me but of my body. It wasn't in great shape. The first problem was my left side. It was numb. Then my head, I could feel the bandage tight over my ear. My right hand was also bandaged. I tried to move my fingers. They worked! Good. I felt better. I wasn't dead, I knew who I was, what had happened, and my hands still worked. That was the bright side. There would be time to deal with the bad side later. Now I needed to get all these people into focus. On closer examination the dozen melted down into five; in the immediate vicinity, an officious young man with a stethoscope, a stunned-looking nurse, an uninterested man in an aggressive raincoat, and—Alex and Nate! I grinned up at the last two.

"Come to dance at my wake, eh? Fooled you," I said with feeble wit. My mouth worked even if my mind wasn't exactly producing gems. Alex Edwards was smiling, a little grimly, but definitely smiling. Nate Ottoline looked concerned and quite unexpectedly tender. The doctor type waved his stethoscope, lifted my eyelid, took my pulse and generally went through the correct motions. The nurse stood by and waited for the great man's verdict.

"Yes, that's quite satisfactory. She can have visitors within reason. Make sure they don't overtire her," he said. "Take it easy with Miss Keremos today, Sergeant," he continued in the direction of the raincoat. "You can see her again tomorrow, if necessary. She should get lots of rest. All right, nurse, let's look at our other patient again."

He and the nurse moved over behind the screen which hid the other half of the room. I couldn't believe the whole production wasn't a scene in a TV hospital show. Especially since it was now clear that the raincoat housed a cop. I turned to Alex and Nate.

"What happened to Sonia? How is she?"

"She's in the bed behind the curtain. She was thrown out of the car by the blast just as you were. They say she'll be OK but it will take time. She's still under sedation. They had to operate."

"Operate? What?"

"Just stitch her up, she got cut. There were some injuries and her right arm is broken in a couple of places." This came from the nameless sergeant, nodding over his notebook. "Now, ladies and gentleman, I would like a few words with Miss Keremos, if you don't mind. Detective Sergeant Malory, Metropolitan Toronto Police. It would be preferable if I saw Miss Keremos alone. I promise not to take long."

Alex looked as if she was about to object. Nate ignored Malory and said, "You OK, Helen? Feel like talking to the Man? Because if not, you sure don't have to."

"Thanks, Nate. No, that's cool. I might as well get it over with."

"Right, we'll be outside. Here's the bell push. Call if you want us for any reason. All right, Sergeant, do your job." They left.

Detective Sergeant Francis Malory was a balding man in his late thirties. He projected that bored self-assurance which is peculiar to big city cops. In spite of the heavy duty image, he turned out to be bright.

"What time is it?" I asked irrelevantly. He glanced at his watch.

"Nine ten."

"Day?"

"A.m. The explosion occurred at 6:48 p.m. last night. You've been here for fourteen hours."

"Oh, that long, eh?"

"Yes, Miss Keremos, let me get this routine over with. You are Helen Keremos, permanently domiciled in Vancouver, BC. Local address, please." I gave him Sonia's apartment hotel. He looked up.

"I understand you have been bodyguarding Miss Sonia Deerfield. You're not a licenced private investigator in Ontario."

"Sergeant, you and I both know that a Private Investigator's licence, so-called, means very little in this jurisdiction. Anyone without a criminal record can get one. It's just a piece of plastic with a picture on it. So what's the odds? I was asked to stay with Miss Deerfield, she's been having problems since she won a large prize in a lottery. Naturally, you know all that by now."

"Yes. Now, we found a gun in the wreckage. An S&W Luger." Just a statement, no comment. Police technique #101. Nuts.

"And you also found a licence for it in my wallet. Issued by the Mounties in British Columbia. Look, Malory, let's cut the crap. We're on the same side. What have you got on the explosion?"

We looked at each other. Our positions were so obviously unequal. There was I, all bandaged up, flat on my back in bed, and there was he, fit and six feet tall. A cop, yet. Cops are trained to intimidate and mystify. Intimidation wasn't working but knowledge is power. Or at least the appearance of power, which cops badly need. Having inside knowledge is great for the old ego.

What line would Sergeant Malory take with me? He could play buddy-buddy and tell me things now which would be public knowledge next day anyway, or he could continue this official bullshit about licences and guns. I figured he would try to get on my right side. He badly needed cooperation. After no more than five seconds of contemplating his options, Malory did the bright thing. He smiled, flipped his notebook back, and told me what I wanted to know.

"Bomb squad figures a small explosive charge was placed between the engine block and the firewall on the driver's side of the vehicle. Don't know how it was triggered yet. Could use your help."

"Well, it wasn't in the ignition and that's one of the simplest ways. No, the engine was running for a good minute before the blast. I tell you what—Sonia was going through the gears— yes, it went off as she got into third."

"But you weren't moving, were you?"

"No, no. Just clutch in at each ratio and back to neutral, clutch out, like that."

"So it could have been the clutch movement which completed the circuit."

"Yes, but it wasn't in first, it was on third or fourth try, I would say."

"Well, I'll tell the bomb boys, see what they make of that. Now, who's trying to kill you? It was you who was the intended victim, right?"

"Yes. Nobody could've known Sonia would be in the car, much less in the driver's seat. She arrived with Lew Davies. But tell me, how come we're alive?"

"Can't tell yet. Perhaps an error. An underestimate."

"Or I wasn't intended to die right there. Let's look at the possibilities. What could anyone assume would happen? Well, that I would be driving and that I wouldn't get into third gear until I was on the road and probably doing forty. Now, if it had happened that way, what would my chances have been?"

"Not good. Would depend on whether you had your seat belt on or not. What saved you this time was that the vehicle was stationary when you were thrown out by the blast. On the road you could have smashed into something. Then, bingo. Also the strength of the fire wall in the truck."

"So it's wide open, that's what we're saying. I may or may not have been intended to die. But certainly the chances were I would be more hurt than I am. And it wasn't meant for Sonia."

"Yes. Now please tell me about your job and about Sonia Deerfield."

"Have you met the bunch that was there at the studio yesterday? Davies, Grelick, Weller—?" I went on with my questions.

"Yes. And Mr. Arthur Sedgwick and Mr. Benjamin Bono. Everyone has already made statements."

"I'll bet. And—?"

"And nothing. Nobody saw or heard anything. Nobody knows anything. Nobody, nothing in fact."

"And you let them get away with that? No ideas who the bomber might be? Did anyone tell you why I was there, why they hired me?"

"Mr. Sedgwick assured us that it had nothing to do with Miss Deerfield's troubles. He was sure that it was someone out of your unsavory past who'd followed you to the studio." Malory and I smiled at each other. Our opinion of Sedgwick and his fairy tale coincided exactly.

"Of course. And because Sedgwick has lots and lots of juice in this town you'll have to investigate me rather than that lot around Sonia. Charming."

"Not quite. We'll investigate both you and Miss Deerfield's entourage. Nothing will be omitted. I'm very, very interested in those 'incidents' that led to your being hired. They weren't reported to us. Mr. Sedgwick Q.C. is on shaky ground on account of that."

"Don't kid me. Shaky ground indeed. Sedgwick could get through the Mexican earthquake without a bump."

Malory didn't answer directly, just pursed his lips in disavowal. I went on impatiently, my head beginning to throb.

"OK, OK. Did anyone mention Walter Lauker to you?"

"You'd better believe it. They all did. Except Sedgwick of course, who is too smart to want any connection to a flake like Lauker. But three of them thought he was the most likely candidate."

"Whom did the others nominate?"

"Oh, each other. Grelick mentioned that Weller was a disbarred lawyer, Bono does not like Karl Deerfield—the usual."

"Have you seen Lauker yet?"

"No, I still have that in store. I understand he's a joy."

"He's an arsehole. But for my money he's clean."

"Yes? We'll see."

Now I could be sure that they'd go over Lauker with a fine tooth comb. Nothing like having the cops do your work for you.

"How about Sonia?" I asked.

"Can't talk to her yet. She's out. Might be a day or two, I'm told. I've been waiting for you to wake up. Now, tell me about your friends. Nate—Ottolinc, is it?"

"I'm sure he's quite well known to some of your downtown boys. He's a friend. Besides, if he wanted to cool me he wouldn't use anything as uncertain as that bomb."

"Hm. And Alex Edwards?"

"An old friend. What d'you expect me to say? Nuts."

"We'll have to investigate them. And you. You know that of course."

"The Mounties will be helpful for starters. And Washington, naturally. Just get on with it, and don't miss anyone."

I looked at my hands. The fingers on my unbandaged hand held traces of black.

"I see you've taken my prints. That's not quite kosher, is it? You had my fingerprints on the gun licence." He looked a mite uncomfortable and promptly denied taking my prints while I was under sedation.

"Never mind lying. I understand. You wanted to find out who I was as fast as possible. One way or another you'll find out a fair bit about me. But zilch about this case. So what good will it do?"

"Routine, just routine. I take it you've been operating in the States. You're an American, then?"

"No, Canadian. But my father was American and I've lived there for a good many years. So?"

"I was only wondering." Malory managed to sound uncertain. "Something like a bombing—and connected to the recording industry—it doesn't sound local."

I laughed out loud.

"Christ, man. You mean it sounds American—organized crime, perhaps! Good clean-living Canucks don't do such things! You've got to be kidding!" Malory stuck to his guns.

"The booking for the session came via Universal Sound. That's a subsidiary of an American 'entertainment' conglomerate. Well, isn't it? It's big, big business. They're into everything. 'Entertainment industry' sort of covers a lot of territory. Certainly organized crime isn't very far away."

This guy had been working, give him credit. Checking up on the booking was smart. But how far could he go?

"Since we're on the subject of connections let me fill you in. Universal Sound is Sedgwick's client in Canada. One of his biggest. That's something to think about. Next, Tri-Met Studio is an 'independent' Canadian company, except that Sedgwick is the biggest stockholder—37%. He controls it. Like it?"

"Not much. These corporate connections give me heartburn."

"Arthur Sedgwick will give you more than heartburn. He'll have you back in uniform. And he'll stay clean. Wanna bet?"

"No." Malory closed his notebook. He'd enough from me to be getting on with. "Well, I guess, you'll be up and about soon. You seem in pretty good form, considering."

"'Bye, Malory. I'm sure we'll be seeing each other soon."

"Bet on it." He had the last word, closing the door behind him.

Early in my conversation with Malory, the medical team had left the room. So now I was alone with Sonia behind the beige hospital curtain. I decided to get up. It wasn't easy. I'd finally gotten shakily to an upright position when Alex and Nate walked in on me.

"What the hell are you doing out of bed?" Alex proceeded to shoo me back under the covers. I obeyed gratefully. I wasn't quite ready to leave my bed, but at least I knew I could stand up.

"OK, I'll be good if you'll fill me in on what's been happening since last night. Alex?"

"Right. Well, your truck's totalled. I called your insurance."

"And now for the bad news, eh? Alex, your bedside manner leaves something to be desired. That's twenty grand worth of truck. Will they pay up in full?"

"I guess so. But your premiums will go up, that's for sure."

"Damn. Well, what else?"

Before Alex or Nate could answer there was a weak sound from the other bed.

"Hello, who's there?" Sonia's voice came over the curtain. Nate stepped forward smartly and drew it aside. Sonia peered out from over bandages and hospital bedclothes. She was smiling feebly, her face a white blur against her red hair. We looked at each other. Perhaps it was shock or a by-product of sedation but she looked happy.

She said, clearer now, "What now, Helen?"

"Now you hurry up and get well. I'll be up and about by tomorrow, get back on the case and clear this mess up double-quick. Don't you worry."

I tried to be more reassuring than I felt. I turned to Alex and Nate again, "By the by, did our brave Sergeant Malory leave a guard here for our protection?"

"There's an overweight young man in the hall outside. But—" Alex answered uncertainly. Nate still hadn't said anything, his attention fixed on the next bed. I introduced them both to Sonia.

"Alex Edwards and Nate Ottoline. Good people. Sonia Deerfield. My client."

"Hello, Sonia. Sorry to meet you in such circumstances. You both need rest, Alex and I must go. We'll be back this afternoon. Meanwhile, I would suggest no visitors," Nate said.

"Ah, the voice of male authority," I kidded but didn't disagree.

17

By NEXT DAY I WAS UP, but Sonia was obviously in for a longer stay. Her personal doctor appeared on the scene and together with the young hospital resident they made the decision to keep her in hospital for at least another two days. After that she could be moved to her apartment accompanied by a nurse.

People visited, sent her flowers, books, clean night clothes, candy, cards. She had a session with Sedgwick and Bono. I don't know what was said but the two lawyers didn't look happy when they left. I was sitting outside Sonia's room with Betty Grelick when Sedgwick passed on his way out.

"Well, it seems we're stuck with each other, Miss Keremos. Sonia insists on retaining your services. Seems redundant to me now that the police are involved but it's her decision. You can count on my full cooperation," he said as graciously as he could.

"That's nice. Incidentally, d'you know where Karl Deerfield is? Everyone else has been to visit Sonia today, but no sign of Uncle Karl."

"I believe he's arranging to move into Sonia's apartment, so he can look after her as soon as she leaves here." Sedgwick was more than pleased to give me that bit of news. "I doubt that there'll be room for you there anymore. Anyway, I'm sure he'll be over presently to tell her about it."

"You mean she wasn't consulted? She doesn't know?"

"That is so. I believe he intends to look after her personal affairs as well since she's incapacitated. As her lawyer I—"

"You do have your nerve, I'll grant you. But you won't get away with it, either of you. Go ahead, have your fun. I'll be around to see you one of these days very soon—to ask a few questions."

"I've already told the police all I know. I've nothing to add."

"I'll be sure to tell Sonia how cooperative you've been."

He shrugged and left. Betty glanced at me and said:

"That's strange about Karl. Not that it isn't a good idea but what makes him think that Sonia will agree to have him take over like that?"

"I don't know. But I'd better find out."

It was time to start work again. My aching body would have to look after itself. I had to think. The routine could be left to the cops. They were trying to narrow down the time when the explosive could have been placed in the truck. Everyone who'd been at Tri-Met that day was being questioned. They were checking times of arrival and departure, comparing stories. There was nothing for me to do in that line. Malory would want to talk to me again as soon as he'd gotten some data about me from the Horsemen and the F.B.I. Then I could pump him about the actual bombing. Of course he would want something in return. You scratch my back, I'll scratch yours. Fair enough.

I had lots to trade. My trump card was my inside track with the people concerned, especially Sonia. I wasn't sure how much pressure it would be safe to put on her at the moment. So if nothing else I had to get to the bottom of Karl's little take-over ploy. As soon as everyone else had left I sat down next to Sonia's bed. She was sitting up a bit now, but couldn't move without pain. She asked me to help her with her hair.

"Brush it for me, would you? I'd rather not have the nurse do it. She talks at me all the time, asks questions. And I don't have anything to say to her. D'you mind?"

I said, no, I didn't mind, but with my arm in a sling I would be clumsy and might hurt her. She shrugged it off. So I got her brush, which Betty had brought from the apartment, and proceeded as carefully as I could to brush her rich, heavy hair. She closed her eyes. Under my strokes her hair came alive, lustre and colour returned, its fullness pulsating through my fingers. I brushed in silence, she appeared to be asleep. Suddenly she spoke, very softly:

"Helen, you know, it's strange. I feel happier here, sick in hospital, than I have for months! It's the first rest I've had for what seems like years. And nothing is expected of me. It's such a relief. I'm not even thinking or worrying about the explosion, or how we got here and all of that. I don't seem to care! Can I just withdraw and let it all go hang?"

I went on stroking gently, deciding how to answer her. She was asking for far more than advice on how to deal with the current situation. She was asking for direction for her whole life. Nothing quick and superficial would do in the long run. But for the present, platitudes would have to do.

"Great that you're happy and great that you're getting this rest. So don't start feeling guilty about that. You've been under a helluva strain so it's natural that reaction should set in."

"Yes, yes I know all that. But what about the future? How do I get out of this mess that my life is in?"

"Don't get morbid on me now. We will get to the bottom of this, find out who's responsible. That'll clear the air. But your life will never be the same again, that's for sure."

"You're saying it's one of them, aren't you? One of my nearest and dearest, one of my friends?"

"Yes, that much is clear. One of the people who were at Tri-Met that day to visit you put that bomb in my truck. It wasn't meant for you but that doesn't change the facts. It's one or more of them who are terrorizing you. I was getting close, or at least someone thought that I might be, and so they decided to take this step. And the bombing removes it from the realm of nuisance or even extortion. That makes it attempted murder. Not even Sedgwick can sweep a bomb under his fancy Persian rug!"

Sonia ignored my crack at Sedgwick. Her mind was still on the main point.

"They were all there. Everyone. Yes, I see. Once it all comes out, no matter who it is, things will never be the same. Meanwhile I can't trust anyone. Except you."

Sonia smiled suddenly, her eyes wide open, green eyes just inches from my face. I stopped brushing. She said:

"Helen, who is it? Who is doing these things? Please find out, please! How can I go on with my life, not knowing?"

There wasn't any point reminding myself not to get emotionally involved. Perhaps I was being manipulated, perhaps it was an act of the kind she'd put across me at our first meeting. It didn't matter, the situation she was in was genuinely ugly. Who can you turn to if you can't trust those closest to you? Her plea arose out of a real need, not self-pity. I touched her shoulder gently.

"For damn sure, you and I'll see this through. See, an attempt like this bomb suggests desperation. Whoever did it is scared, close to the brink. It makes them dangerous but also vulnerable. For one thing, all the usual relationships, routines, dynamics have been disrupted. It's like a kaleidoscope being turned. Everything looks different, odd things pop up out of the background, hidden things show up. People lose perspective, do unexpected things, give themselves away. Like your Uncle Karl. He's trying to move into your apartment while you're here in hospital."

I'd expected a reaction from Sonia at this but nothing on the scale of what occurred.

"Oh my god, no. Helen, no! I can't have him there. It's the last straw. No! No!" Sonia was beside herself, her face contorted, full of pain and fear.

"Take it easy, take it easy! It isn't going to happen. Management won't let him in without your personal sayso. I've talked to their security man. He's an old buddy of mine, sort of. So take hold of yourself and tell me why this freakout. Karl isn't my idea of a desirable room mate, but—"

I stopped. Sonia was shaking. I sat down on the edge of the bed, took her hand and said as calmly as I could:

"Tell me. Tell me now."

"All right. Yes, it'll be good to get it out. Reach me a tissue, will you. It's in the table beside you."

I handed her a tissue and waited as she got herself together, blew her nose, wiped her eyes before continuing:

"We lived in Owen Sound when I was small. My father worked for the post office. I was born in 1952 and one of the first things I remember was how everyone said what a big deal my Uncle Karl was. He'd been a war hero, you see. My mother adored him, my father seemed to be in awe of him. He had medals and a commission in the Engineers, while my father never made it past PFC and never saw any action. So my Uncle Karl could do no wrong. Well, when I was about eight he started, well, you know—molesting me."

Slowly and painfully Sonia told me her story. She'd accepted Karl's use of her body as just another thing to put up with from authoritarian adults. Life was like that. An eight-year-old had to go along with demands from teachers, parents, neighbours and relatives. Karl wasn't particularly rough or abusive; the initial painfulness soon passed. She didn't much like what was happening but then she hadn't much liked other things she was forced to do. Growing up in small town Ontario in the fifties could be an ordeal for a young girl. Sonia was eager to please. She became adept at all the many little ways it took to get approval. She adapted and was considered a sweet, obedient, pretty little girl.

She was aware that what Uncle Karl did to her and with her must not be talked about. He, of course, stressed that it was a little secret between them, making it special. Karl was a powerful adult in her life, his attentions, his good will weren't lightly to be endangered. So she went along, 'consented'.

It was her younger sister who finally blew the affair wide open. She was envious of all the attention her older sister was getting from their wonderful Uncle Karl. She too wanted trips in his car, hikes along the Georgian Bay cliffs, the ice cream and toys with which Karl never failed to reward Sonia. She spotted something untoward between Sonia and Karl and although not understanding, knew that a threat to 'tell' would have a powerful effect. Things happened very fast after that. Karl promptly left town, leaving Sonia to deal with her mother. Sonia had expected to be punished but had no inkling of what in fact happened. At first her mother would not believe her and made both girls promise not to tell anyone. Then she blamed Sonia for everything. Her beloved brother Karl couldn't have done anything wrong and must have been seduced by an eight-year-old! This fantasy seemed easier to take than the reality of what her brother had done.

From that time on Sonia effectively lost her mother. That unfortunate woman wasn't capable of handling the competing loyalties to her brother and her eldest daughter. She accepted Karl's explanation— "I couldn't help myself"—and totally rejected Sonia, making her into the evil temptress. When at fourteen Sonia was picked up drunk by the Ontario Provincial Police in a car with two local boys, her mother's self-fulfilling judgment on Sonia as a sinful female was confirmed. The following year, unable to stand her life in Owen Sound, Sonia took a bus to Toronto. No one bothered to look for her. It was 1967, the sixties were in full swing.

As she told me this sad familiar tale, Sonia's voice strengthened. Towards the end the tears were gone and her face was set with a mask of anger.

"Now I understand what a terrible thing was done to me. Not the physical part, that wasn't as bad as lots I experienced after I came to Toronto, believe me. But the guilt that was laid on me, the rejection! I still have moments of feeling that I deserved the treatment I got. I've had to fight this self-hatred all these years. All because of him. I'll never forgive him, never! Do you understand?"

"Yes, I understand."

"I can't stand the sight of him, can't bear to have him near me. As for having him live with me, having him there among my things, in my apartment even when I'm away! Never!"

"Yes, I understand," I repeated. Then hastened to reassure her that Karl would not set foot in her place.

"Call the manager if you like, and personally confirm that you don't want Karl in your place. That'll put paid to his whole crazy idea."

"Do you think he could be crazy? Really? I've wondered in the last little while. You know, he sort of appeared again in my life a couple of years ago, after my mother died. He seems just a bumbling, foolish, old man now. We never talked about the past, I never see him alone or invite him up to my place.

That's why I was so stunned when I found him there with you the other day."

"That must've been a shock. I'm sorry. I'd no idea. As you say, he seemed just an amiable bore. As to whether he's crazy, that depends on what you mean by crazy. Anyway, tomorrow I'll be out of here, I'll deal with him. OK?"

Sonia agreed gratefully. She'd had enough. I handed her two ASAs and she finally fell asleep.

I didn't sleep for a long, long time.

18

OVER A BLAND HOSPITAL BREAKFAST Sonia and I conferred. Nothing more was said about Karl Deerfield. Instead we went over the very simple scheme I'd cooked up overnight.

Sonia was to let it be known that she was ready to settle with the extortionist/bomber. Pay up some reasonable amount to be left alone. Keeping the cops out of it, naturally. The idea was to make it safe for whomever was responsible to make a specific demand, knowing in advance that it would be accepted. To make it easier, Sonia was to get herself back to her apartment as soon as possible. It was obvious to any idiot that the hospital phone was monitored by the cops. So her immediate task was to sign out of hospital and make herself accessible.

I said goodby to Sonia and was leaving the hospital when Ben Bono and Lew Davies arrived. I'd never seen them together or thought of them in combination among the people surrounding Sonia. Each belonged in a separate category. Curious, I stuck around.

Sonia wasn't ready to receive them yet, so the three of us hung out together in a small waiting area a few doors from her room. Plastic chairs, an old black and white TV and ancient magazines. We started discussing Sonia's injuries, moved on to mine. Ben Bono commented sympathetically on my bruises just starting to turn yellow. The conversation continued in this vein, nothing real getting said. Ben Bono, natty in discreet pin stripes, paced the room, nervously chain smoking. Lew Davies sat picking lint off his sleeves. Conversation flagged until Bono mentioned the guard outside. He was a twin of the overweight cop of the day before except that his socks were white.

"Helen, how well do you think are the cops protecting Sonia? That guy outside doesn't seem enough."

"I wouldn't worry. Sonia wasn't the intended victim of the

bomber in the first place. It's true that guard couldn't really prevent an attempt on her life but he does make it somewhat more difficult. That's really all the cops can do. The assumption is that the bomber isn't crazy and wouldn't take the risk."

"What about you, then? Aren't you vulnerable to another attempt?" That was Davies. A reasonable question.

"Sure I'm vulnerable. But you don't expect me to go around in tandem with a cop bodyguard, do you? And that wouldn't be much use if someone really intended to get me. A rifle from across the street—"

"But you're staying on the case, aren't you? In spite of the danger."

"You better believe it." I put on my most valiant face, making it hurt.

"Very commendable," said Bono. "But I don't see what's in it for you. Why are you doing this?"

Now was the time to push this conversation over the edge. So I answered, "I could as well ask, why are you bird-dogging for Sedgwick when you want Sonia for yourself?" They both stared at me uncomprehendingly, then Bono reacted, "What! What do you mean 'bird-dogging for Sedgwick'? What are you suggesting?"

"Come, come. Are you really unaware that you're used by the great man, and how? Would he really be involved with Sonia Deerfield to this extent if she was a mere client? Sure, getting Universal Sound interested in contracting Sonia might be good business. But is that all Sedgwick wants? Ask yourself, do you know of any other client in Sonia's class that he takes so much time and trouble with?"

"But—" Bono stopped pacing and looked at me. The sleepless circles under his dark eyes seemed to deepen as the possible implications of what I'd said sunk in. I pressed on.

"Remember how it all started? Go on. Tell us how Sedgwick became involved."

"All right. I saw Sonia performing downstairs at the El Mocambo one night. She was...great. I guess I fell in love with her right there and then. We met and started to go out together.

I kept following her to all her gigs. Then Arthur came with me to one of them. Just by chance. He thought she was too good for the places she was working at, that she needed a first-class manager." He stopped again, turned to Davies and continued excitedly. "Then it happened very fast, right Lew? Sedgwick turned up Chuck Weller—yes—got Sonia to hire him, and has been in on the scene all the time since—yes. Wow!"

I picked up on the point.

"Sedgwick has Weller in his pocket. He's Weller's passport back to respectability, to a job, a position. By controlling Weller, he controls Sonia. He's been orchestrating every move ever since. Those 'better' gigs Sonia's been getting lately. Whose influence has that been? Sure as hell not Weller's. He's just the front man."

Bono got a hold on himself, control of his voice. He wasn't buying this scenario without an argument.

"All right, you made your point. Except for motive. What are you suggesting are Arthur's intentions vis-à-vis Sonia? He's married, has children and is old enough to be her father."

"That fooled you, did it? How conventional of you. But you know Sedgwick. What is his most outstanding personal characteristic? What does he care about most? It's certainly not his marriage, that's for sure. Well?"

Before Bono could reply, Davies broke in, right on the money:

"He's a collector! Yes, Sedgwick is a collector of beautiful things. He works at getting what he wants. Ben, she could be right!"

"Of course! A collector of beauty! I never thought of it that way. But it's true. And Sonia is the most beautiful woman—"

There was a moment of silence with the three of us carefully avoiding each other's eyes. Volumes went unsaid about our feelings for Sonia. Bono was the first to speak:

"It's hard to believe. I guess I've always looked up to Arthur. He's been my mentor, my friend. You know, it wasn't easy for a Wop like me to break into the big time. The old boys network, you know. They all went to private schools and married each other's sisters. Arthur helped me, hired me, taught me the ropes, recommended me for a partnership. I'm grateful."

"Oh, Ben. You were hand-picked! There're 400,000 Italians in Toronto. They run the construction industry. An operator like Sedgwick knows how useful a smart, ambitious paisan can be. You earn your keep."

"All right, I earn my keep! I deserve my place in the firm. But he's been good to me. We are friends. It isn't all just a front!"

"Perhaps. But only as long as you stay in line. Remember that. Sedgwick made you, you say so yourself. He made you and he made you grateful. Just as he's 'making' Sonia, getting to own her, to control her life—"

At this Davies burst out:

"We don't need him. Sonia and I don't need any of you! Not you, Ben, or Sedgwick or Weller. With our talents and her million we can do anything. The hell with you all!"

"Ah, at last. That million. Amazing how it gets forgotten. Yet every so often it does get mentioned. Which brings us back to the threats and the bomb. Tell me, Ben, how did Sedgwick react when Sonia won all that money?" I asked.

"He didn't like it. I don't know how to put it but now that you mention it he was, well, disturbed. Then after a while it was business as usual, I guess," Bono answered.

"It didn't fit his plans at all. With Sonia financially independent, she didn't need him. Lew is quite right there, of course. But Sedgwick is such a powerful personality that he managed to have all of you overlook the implications of that wealth. 'Business as usual' means Sedgwick still running things."

"So Sedgwick got Walter Lauker to threaten Sonia! To make her hate her money and get her to turn to him for help. And the bomb—" Davies said. Ben Bono would have none of it:

"I don't believe it. I just don't. Is that what you think, Helen?" But I wasn't ready to tell them what I thought.

"It's an interesting possibility. But there are others. All just speculation at the moment. Well, gentlemen, it's been stimulating but I must go. I've an appointment with Detective Sergeant Malory. I'm sure that by the time I get to it he'll have heard about our session here from the watchdog outside. You must expect another interrogation. Malory will want to know what we talked about."

"What do you suggest we tell the cops?" Davies asked. "What are you going to tell Malory?"

"Well, generally it's best to tell the truth. Not to volunteer anything but answer questions as truthfully as possible under the circumstances. It's safer and less of a strain on the memory. Unless of course you've something badly discreditable to hide. I'm sure that Ben would agree. As a lawyer, wouldn't you agree, Ben?"

"Yes, of course. Truth as one knows it. But it's not at all necessary to share one's speculation or opinions with the police. That is never indicated. The correct procedure is to answer factual questions about oneself. What, when, where. That sort of thing."

"See, Lew? Free advice from a top-notch lawyer. Good advice, too. I'm on my way. Don't tire Sonia, you two. She needs her rest."

I hobbled out past the watchful guard, picked up my few things and left the hospital.

19

Malory was hiding out in a cluttered room at Metropolitan Toronto Police headquarters, a building which still looks much like the head office of the insurance company it was designed for. I sat down and was offered coffee. I was trying to decide where it belonged in my private pantheon of awful office coffees when another man joined us.

Superintendent Sterling was a grey man with a well worn sad face and cold blue eyes. It flashed through my mind that he and Sedgwick had much in common, even across the gulf of wealth and class. This first impression was confirmed during the course of the interview. Sterling said very little. He let Malory ask almost all the questions. But his presence was heavy in the room. Every word which Malory and I spoke apparently to each other was said with our audience in mind.

After the short introduction and routine inquiries about the state of my and Sonia's health, Malory picked up a file, glancing through it in a studied, casual manner.

He began, "Miss Keremos, I have here information about you and a number of other people connected with this case. Would you mind filling in some of the gaps?"

"Fire away. What do you want to know?"

"First about the explosion itself. We're now working on the assumption that the bomb was placed in your truck sometime between one and four that afternoon. There wasn't anyone at the parking lot gate during that time. The attendant was away for lunch from 1 to 2 p.m. and shortly after that was called away home on an urgent family matter. That turned out to be a false alarm. In any case he didn't get back until 4 p.m. So apart from the odd person coming and going through the parking lot there was no one there for those three hours. Strictly speaking anyone could've just walked in, placed the bomb in your vehicle and gotten out again. It needn't have been one of the people who visited Tri-Met that afternoon.

In view of this we must explore the possibility that the explosion which was clearly meant for you wasn't connected with the case you're currently on but rather arose out of something in your past. You see my point?"

"I see your point all right. The department would rather that it had nothing to do with Mr. Arthur Sedgwick. I sympathize. But it won't work. I didn't know myself until that morning where I was going to be and not until the night before that there was a recording session at all. Are you suggesting that someone followed me around with a pre-prepared explosive device on the off chance that they would have the opportunity to pop it into my truck? Who are you suggesting would operate like that?"

While I spoke, Malory flipped through the file.

"Well, you do have a very varied background going back to the late fifties. Mostly in the States." Malory moved his hand down a sheet in his file as if reading from it. "...After a stint in U.S. Naval security disappeared, whereabouts unknown. Next noted working for a detective agency in California... There could be organized crime connections there...moved to eastern Canada mid-sixties...presumably continued undercover work...many trips to Montreal, New York, Boston... Just what were you doing then, Miss Keremos?"

"No, Sergeant. This act of yours is very impressive but you must first show the relevance of your questions to the present case. No fishing expeditions. You forgot to mention that in 1971 I returned to Vancouver and set up as a private investigator. Mounties checked me out then and presumably gave me a clean bill since I got a licence and a gun permit. So as far as Toronto police are concerned I'm a regular law-abiding citizen with every right to make a living. Your dark hints of American-sponsored Mafia connections are out of line. They are ludicrous, in fact. As I'm sure you're well aware. You boys had better face the fact that you've a nasty case on your hands involving a leading citizen of this province, one Arthur Sedgwick. I quite understand that he has lots of juice and he's been using every bit of it to head you off this case. I understand your problem. All the same, try to deal from the top of the deck. You can't hope to get away with pushing this affair onto my gory past. What have you found out about others in this case?"

Malory glanced at his superior, sighed and answered:

"Not a great deal. Apart from Weller and Lauker they are all more or less solid citizens. Sedgwick is spotless and so is Bono. Grelick was once a found-in under the Liquor Act, as who wasn't, and Davies owes alimony to his ex-wife, as who doesn't. That's all. They are exactly as they seem. Middling successful, well known but not notorious in their field. Karl Deerfield. Owen Sound police reports him as a bit of a nut, details unknown. That doesn't mean a lot coming from a small town like that."

Like most metropolitan cops, Malory was a big-city chauvinist to his fingertips. He continued:

"Deerfield still owns a gas station there, but doesn't run it day-to-day. Seems to be in semi-retirement since he left the Department of Highways a few years back. Now Weller is a case, definitely a case. He and Sedgwick were classmates at Osgoode Hall law school, took their bar exams together. But Sedgwick is Upper Canada College and a Rosedale mansion, while Weller just managed to make it up from a Parkdale slum. Guess he took too many short cuts, got caught with his hand in a client's trust account. He didn't have the heavy backing necessary to get through the Law Society, so got himself disbarred. Now his old friend Sedgwick seems to be giving him a hand up with this job as manager for Sonia Deerfield. Nothing there for us." Malory stopped.

"You guys aren't a bit subtle. Of course Sedgwick is squeaky clean. He has the likes of Weller doing his dirty work for him. The same is true of every major law firm in this city. You know it, I know it. So what is this charade in aid of?"

At this point Sterling finally opened his mouth.

"Miss Keremos, I could ask you the same thing. What are you trying to suggest? That Mr. Sedgwick got Mr. Weller to place a bomb in your vehicle? There is no evidence or motive for such an action on his part. We would be delighted if you would provide us with any real leads. I promise they will be followed up. But you can't expect us to pursue a man of Mr. Sedgwick's reputation on mere speculation."

"There's motive all right, although you may not think so. Getting rid of me. I was getting to be a nuisance."

"Come, come, Miss Keremos. You must be aware that Mr. Sedgwick doesn't need to dispose of nuisances by blowing them up. There are half a dozen ways he could've removed you from Miss Deerfield's employ if he cared to do that."

"Not without it showing. Sedgwick is a suspect precisely because a bomb is so out of character for him. No one, not Sonia, not you, would ever suspect him."

Sterling gave a well controlled laugh.

"I'm afraid, Miss Keremos, that is too far-fetched for us. Do you have anything specific and concrete against Mr. Sedgwick? If so, tell us."

"I don't, but I bet you do. Otherwise, why worry what I know or suspect? Neither he nor Weller has an alibi for those hours, right?"

Malory answered:

"Only Miss Deerfield and Lew Davies seem to be out of it at the moment. They were in the studio working in plain view of a number of people all the time. Sedgwick and Weller don't have alibis but that means nothing."

"Nothing means anything except in the right context. So who've you got picked out? You haven't mentioned Walter Lauker yet."

"Yes. Walter Lauker. He has had a few run-ins with us. Pulled in on suspicion of possession of stolen goods. Insufficient evidence. A few other minor offences, one conviction. Impersonating a police officer. Got away with a small fine. Definitely unstable, liable to do anything."

It was my turn to snigger.

"So you like him for the bombing. No wonder. But that is a heavy trip. One moment you're all hot for some Mafia connection, next you finger a stray nut like Lauker. What's it to be? Is this serious or is this serious?"

"Oh, it's serious all right. We will explore all possibilities. I take it then, Miss Keremos, that you believe we would be remiss not to investigate Mr. Weller more thoroughly? As a real possibility. If there's any conspiracy between him and Mr. Sedgwick we'll certainly find it. Satisfied?" That was Sterling, of course.

"Nothing will satisfy me until we get the guy who did it. Pull Weller in and have a go at him, by all means. Interesting to see how Sedgwick will react to having his protégé under suspicion."

"Indeed. Very interesting. It's been a pleasure, Miss Keremos. Thank you for your cooperation."

Sterling gave me a neat nod and left. Malory and I looked at each other. Finally I spoke:

"Let me guess. The brass upstairs haven't decided how to play this case. Whether it has to be a major event or whether it might be possible to play it down. Sterling was here to check me over, to see if they have any option. Now it's clear they don't. I won't let them bury this. So you'll go after Weller and even Sedgwick, if necessary. How am I doing?"

"No comment," Malory grinned. I grinned back and got out of there. I knew I'd been a big help to Malory. And that wasn't bad news at all.

20

MY NEXT STOP was Nate's. Ronnie greeted me like a long-lost friend, found me a beer and was solicitous to a fault. Not so Nate. He glared at me from over his inevitable cigar.

"Are you nuts?" he asked. "Why didn't you split this town when the going was good? Getting mixed up with this caper! It's dynamite!" He had the grace to grin at the bad pun. "I've already had the cops sniffing around me, and I'm not even involved. Do you know what the climate is in this city right now? This could put me out of business. You, you don't live here, you've nothing to lose."

"Yeah. Nothing to lose except my truck and almost my life. A bomb yet! Who could've predicted that. I can't quit now, that's for sure."

Nate sighed heavily. "Oh, hell. So what do you want from me?"

"Nate, you're a prince," I said. He made another face. "OK, not a prince. Choose your title." I was much relieved and grateful. Nate would come through. It was good to know. "I need the real scoop on Sedgwick and Universal Sound. Something smells there. I know there's a connection but how deep does it go? Deep enough so he would need to use a bomb to get rid of me?"

"I knew you would want Sedgwick. How about the Mayor? It would be easier and much less risky. All right, I'll do what I can. Anything else?"

"Grelick and Davies. Anything at all on them. Malory says they are just what they seem. Are they?"

"I know a little. It may help. Grelick does OK in a small way as a booking agent. But it must be a struggle. She and Davies were making it at one time but that seems to have faded. No hard feelings as far as anyone knows. They are both very attached to Sonia; but you know that."

"Why would she want to scare Sonia and where would she

get the knowhow and the explosives to make that device?"

Nate shrugged his shoulders.

"Can't answer that. Motive is for you to figure out. But I can think of a reason or two why she might want you out of Sonia's life. Personal reasons. Admittedly a bomb is a bit drastic. As to where she might have gotten it—no way of telling. Toronto isn't a terrorist hotbed but you can get anything you want here if you know the ropes. She knows a lot of people here. And in Montreal and New York for that matter."

"Which all adds up to big fat nothing. Now, how about Davies?"

"Much the same. Arrived from the UK back in the sixties, like a lot of them broke into the CBC right away. Did OK, good pianist, arranger. Had a staff job for a while. Came the cutbacks he went freelance. Hooked up with Sonia on some gig or other. Owns a small townhouse in Cabbagetown, divorced, one child, no known attachments at the moment. Appears to be straight. Used to teach at a community college for mortgage money, quit when Sonia won and put him on the payroll fulltime."

"Expensive tastes?"

"Buys coke. Scuttlebutt has it that he dropped close to ten grand on the white stuff in the last while."

"Can he afford that?"

"He can now, if he's careful. Sonia pays him thirty. Freelance work plus residuals on some commercials he worked on, he does OK."

"That won't go far if he's into coke in a big way. He owes child support. Know anything about his ex-wife?"

"No, but I can find out."

"Do that. How about Lauker?"

"Lauker. You know, I don't really know about Lauker. He's so obvious. It could all be an illusion. Flamboyant, a little nuts...he could be anything under all that."

"Yes, a good facade. Could be. Unlikely, though. You know anyone who could carry that kind of front off consistently?"

"But he's not consistent. That's what makes him so interesting. Can be tough and knowledgeable when he needs to be. Cops think he's a fence in a minor way."

"What do you think?"

"Sure, it's true. So what? It's just another cover."

"That's a bit convoluted. You don't like him."

"I don't know him, not really. We have done some business, that's all. I don't trust him."

"How about him and Sonia. He's crazy about her still, right?"

"Everyone is crazy about Sonia. Look at you." He leered exaggeratedly. Then he lit a fresh cigar and offered me another drink. I declined. My body ached in all the old familiar places. Ronnie got me a cab and I went to Sonia's apartment to rest. Considering all the bits and pieces of information I'd picked up buzzing in my sore head it didn't take me long to fall asleep.

Three hours later a ring on my private line brought me up from a dark dream. I tried to hold on to it but it fled as I fought towards consciousness. Somehow it had seemed significant as dreams often do after the fact. I sat for a moment letting the phone ring, trying to remember. Then gave up and answered. It was the insurance adjustor. The cops had let him see the remains of my beautiful 4X4. He wanted to see invoices for all the extra communication equipment I had had installed. I said I would send him copies by courier. He was polite and curious about the explosion. Said there would be no problem getting very close to full value. I muttered something ungracious and hung up. It bugs me when insurance companies act as if they were doing you a favour to pay up what you have coming.

The short sleep had done me good. I felt rested enough to think. Then the phone rang again. This time it was Sonia. She'd just had a visit from Sedgwick. He'd arrived just as Bono and Davies were leaving and there had been a dust-up between Sedgwick and Bono. I said I could imagine there would be. Sonia wasn't interested. As we had planned, she told them all that she was ready to deal and was only waiting for another phone call to arrange the pay-off. None of them had commented. It had been a very strange and tense meeting altogether.

Once the two younger men had left, Sedgwick put on a heavy act for Sonia. Quite out of character, according to her; she had never seen him except in his all-knowing fatherly role. He informed her that Universal Sound wanted a contract immediately. He insisted that it would be the very best she could hope to get but had to be signed right away or the opportunity would be lost forever. It sounded as phony as a three dollar bill, even to Sonia. She'd pointed out very reasonably that the demo tape wasn't completed, that she was still ill and in no shape to make any such commitment. Sedgwick waved all that aside. He was most insistent she sign right away. He stayed and pressured her for twenty minutes until in her weakened state she started to cry, called a nurse and ordered him out. What did I make of that, she now asked me.

"Nothing, specifically. He's under some sort of pressure." I was trying to make sense of this turn of events myself. "What else?"

"He gave me until tomorrow to make up my mind. Take it or leave it. And he was very bitter against you. Said it was all your doing, that it had been a mistake to hire you. You were a troublemaker." I laughed.

"That's true. And a good thing too. Now you should have someone to stay with you, besides your watchdog that is. To keep those bastards from getting to you this way. How about I call Betty and get her to keep you company?"

"Betty? Oh, she's here now. So that's OK Helen, Ben and Lew also acted pretty strange when they were visiting me, even before Arthur showed up. I've never seen Ben so uptight." I told her not to worry. We hung up, promising to be in touch soon.

I sat on my bed thinking about Sedgwick and the Universal Sound contract, wondering what the scam could be. Idly I looked over at the half-opened door to the living room. A movement behind it caught my eye. Someone was in the next room. Carefully I lifted my ass off the bed and crept softly towards the door. Just as I reached it there was the sound of quick movement and I heard the apartment door open. I quit faking it and ran in as a dark shape disappeared, and by the time I made it out to the corridor there was no sign of the intruder. The bright EXIT light glowed red over the door to the stairwell. Racing towards it, and through it, I tried to attune my ears to sounds of footsteps other than my own. Silence. Looking both ways, up and down, I couldn't see past the first turn in the narrow cement stairs. It was a toss-up which direction the intruder had taken. I kept on running down figuring that even if that wasn't the right direction I could still get to the exits first and prevent escape. Maybe. On the other hand, there was no point going up unless I could be sure that was the way the intruder had gone. There was nothing wrong with my logic given the choices. When I reached the lobby all three elevators were in use on upper floors. Chester, the house dick, was talking to a serious-looking elderly gent in a too-tight business suit. Giving him the high sign I made for the rear exits. Through the kitchens, to the delivery and hotel entrance. The polyglot sounds of the hotel staff followed me. So, finally, did Chester.

"Hey, what gives?" he asked, more amused than concerned.

"Creeper in the Deerfield apartment. I think I lost him. Damn, I know I did. You seen anyone?"

"You kidding? I've seen a dozen. Who are we looking for?"

"I don't know. I don't think anyone left this way but we would never know if anyone had. Damn. Let's go talk to the desk clerk in the lobby."

No use. It was a busy evening. People in and out. No one noticed anything. No one was seen to run out. A total bust.

Chester and I consoled ourselves with a drink from his office bottle in a closet-sized 'Security Office'. I didn't want to give up.

"OK, he just walked out. Like any upstanding citizen. But what if he hasn't? How many check-ins have you had today?"

"Sixteen. Mostly single males. Want a peek at the register?

About half are regulars. Don't know any of the others. How do you know it's today's check-in?"

"I don't but it's worth a try. What've we got to lose? Let's get out there and have the clerk point them out. The strangers. Who was in during the last half hour?"

Chester sighed and reached for the house phone. After lengthy negotiations he established that five of the freshly checked-in single males were not known to be out. So probably they were in the hotel at the significant time. Probably. Possibly. Maybe.

It wasn't worth following up. I went back to Sonia's apartment and checked it over. Nothing was missing or disarranged that I could spot. I found no bomb, no foreign object of any kind.

I put in time calling Malory to inquire about the recent whereabouts of our favourite suspects. On hearing about the uninvited visitor to Sonia's apartment he almost spat at me over the phone.

"Stay where you are," he shouted. "I'll be right over." I told him I hadn't planned on going anywhere but he was off the line. Sitting and waiting for the long arm of the law, I mulled over the possibilities. It could have been a coincidence, nothing to do with the explosion or the phone threats. I couldn't sell myself that one. The prowler and the extortionist had to be intimately related, probably one and the same. And I still liked the idea of it being a hotel resident. Maybe a regular whom nobody noticed any more. Probably, possibly, maybe.

Twenty minutes later Malory and an underling arrived, accompanied by Chester who scowled at me, not appreciating the company we were keeping. Police are not good for hotel business. Having obviously already pumped him dry, Malory now ignored Chester and started in on me. Who, what, where, how? What had I seen, what was I doing, what had I done? Then he and the silent cop went over the apartment all over again. Searches by civilians like me do not count. But they too came up empty.

Malory finally chose to simmer down. He lit a cigarette and

said, "So what have we got? Nothing I can see. Just a prowler. A coincidence?"

"If you believe in the tooth fairy," I said.

"Right. I don't buy coincidence, either. But we still don't know who it was. Only who it wasn't!" Malory allowed himself a little grin at my expense. "It wasn't Weller, that's who it wasn't. We pulled him in for questioning just like you suggested at our little talk earlier in the day. So much for that idea. Unless you believe that for a change Sedgwick was doing his own dirty work, whatever it was."

"No. Sedgwick wouldn't pick locks," I answered. "But he was very concerned about Weller getting picked up and questioned. He's been trying to pressure Sonia, hurrying things along, like he was afraid something would break before he'd gotten her all signed up. Any guesses about that? Did you get anything out of Weller?"

"Some. Nothing directly relevant to the bombing." Malory was being cagy but I couldn't tell if he had anything to be cagy about or whether it was just habit. "We'll check all the other suspects, see where they were in the past two hours. Perhaps that will narrow things down."

Thinking as he talked, I said, "Karl Deerfield has been trying to get access to this apartment. It could've been him."

"Deerfield? Wouldn't they spot him downstairs?"

"Not necessarily. He looks like a million other middle-aged men. They wouldn't connect him with Sonia."

"So you like Deerfield for the prowler, eh Helen? D'you like him for the bomber, too?" Malory asked.

Suddenly I was sure. I said, "Yes, I like him for that. Let's go talk to him."

But Malory wouldn't bite.

"You talk to him if you're so keen. I've got a mountain of paper work to do, and these alibis to check. We had to let Weller go, you know. Nothing on him."

"Good, I'll talk to both of them myself," I said. That ended the session. I walked out.

21

IT WAS DARK. I stood outside the hotel debating how to proceed. As usual in such cases there wasn't time to go over everything thoroughly, to make careful plans, to cover all options and contingencies. All I had going for me was a feeling of urgency; it hadn't left me since I woke up and couldn't remember that dream. Maybe it hadn't been a dream that had so disturbed me; in my sleep I might have become aware of the prowler in the next room. Whatever it had been, now the feeling wouldn't leave me. My arm ached. Taking it out of the sling I flexed my hand and shoulder. Indifferent to the stares of passersby I jogged on the spot for a few moments. My body worked but my mind remained all fogged up. Was I behaving rationally? Walking out on Malory like that in pursuit of Karl Deerfield. What reason did I have to think he was the bad guy? Perhaps it was only my reaction to Sonia's story about her childhood? It would be nonsense to deny the influence of emotion on my perceptions. I believed my reasons were sound but I couldn't be sure.

So now what? Whether 'objectively' I was right or not, I had to see Deerfield. There were half a dozen places I could start looking for him. If he'd been the prowler, where would he have gone afterwards? Home? His address in Toronto was a rented room not far from the hotel where I stood. I stepped back into the lobby and called. A gruff male voice answered. Deerfield wasn't in and hadn't been seen all day. I hung up. How about the hospital? Betty was there with Sonia, and it was after visiting hours. Doubtful. Of course, he could be in a bar or almost anywhere else in town. But his room was still the best bet. I wondered if the cops had been over it. I decided it was unlikely. I walked over to the old, rundown building. A sign said: 'Rooms by day or week. Men only.' So it was that sort of place. Interesting.

On the porch a couple of winos stared blankly at me.

"Deerfield. What's his room number?" I asked.

"Whoa!" One of them decided to be difficult. "Who wants to know? Who the hell are you?"

It's dull sitting on a porch watching people go past. I would've liked to oblige him with my company but I didn't think I could hack this particular scene right then. It was too reminiscent of my early years on Vancouver's Main Street strip. My mother ended up an alcoholic. When she wasn't hustling for the price of a bottle she spent her time on a porch very much like this, with other alkies very much like these. So I replied, "His truant officer. What's it to you?"

The man broke up at this tired old sally.

"His truant officer!! Ha, ha. Wait 'til I tell the boys! Hey, Fred, there's a dyke looking for the General. His truant officer, she says! Ha!"

He nudged his companion who said, "The General is out. Inspecting the troops. If you want his H.Q. try the Imperial Palace Hotel." Both of them laughed and looked up at me expectantly. I nodded.

"I just came from there. Want to get something from his room. What's the number?"

"Sixteen. But there's nothing there. We know, we looked. Not a drop. Cheap bastard."

"Well, that's a General for you," I said. "Thanks," and I left them still giggling happily to themselves.

Karl Deerfield's room was like others I've seen in buildings like this—small, mean, dirty and almost empty. I went through it quickly. It wasn't an easy or particularly pleasant search. The bed was unmade. It smelled. There was some soap and shaving gear, a couple of coats in the closet, a clean shirt or two and very little else. I went through the coat pockets. Nothing. I stripped the bed clothes, gingerly. Nothing. Bottom of drawers, behind the mirror. Nothing. Finally all that was left was the waste container—an old 5-gallon paint can. There, among weeks' accumulation of crud I found a crumpled Imperial Palace Hotel room receipt. Made out to Captain K. Demarest. Three days at $68 per day. Dates covered the day

Sonia's apartment was vandalized a few weeks ago.

There was adrenalin in my system and a zip in my step as I made my way down to the musky lobby. This proved to be bad luck for the unhealthy-looking youngish man in a green work shirt with 'Merv' embroidered over the left breast pocket. He accosted me by the front door. My two previous acquaintances from the front porch stood behind him expectantly. They had obviously sicked him on to me hoping for a little excitement. Merv was drunk and nasty. "We don't allow no broads in here. What you doing with the General's room? Goddam whores!"

"Piss off," I countered elegantly and made to push past him through the door. His shoulder blocked my way, his hand grabbed my arm. It was my bad arm. It hurt. Without a moment's thought I lashed out my undamaged arm simultaneously kicking his knee. The side of my hand connected with a satisfying thump. He fell backwards and lay holding the side of his face. Our audience immediately switched sides. They were with the winner all the way. No liberal shit about supporting the underdog about them.

"Good on you lady! Give it to him, the sod."

"Hey, man! What's it like down there? Fucking serves you right, you bleeding pimp."

It went on but I didn't wait to hear. I had things to do and people to see. Almost running from that dreary, unhappy place I made my way to the nearest phone. I tried Lew Davies.

"I want Karl Deerfield. Where is he?" My urgency was plain.

"Why Karl? I thought you were after Sedgwick. Hey, I liked that number you did on Bono this morning. That really started something. Looks like Sedgwick will lose his boy. Congratulations."

"Never mind all that. What do you know about Karl Deerfield?"

"What's to know? He hangs around. That's all."

"'Hangs around'? Where? Have you ever seen him at Sonia's hotel?"

"Yes. No. I don't know. He's been underfoot lately. That's all I know. Why?" he repeated.

"Thanks. 'Bye." I hung up.

Next Weller. He wasn't at home. After some persuasion his wife said she thought he might be at the Hot Shot Club, a members-only hangout for broadcasters and sports freaks. It too was on Jarvis Street. I walked. He was there, all right. With Bono. Ben Bono looked angry and out of place among the solidly Anglo turtleneck-and-blazer crowd in the upstairs bar. Weller just sat there drinking scotch. His eyes weren't focusing. Neither was overjoyed to see me but Bono was talking and couldn't stop.

"I'm through. Hear me, Weller? Through! Sedgwick and Company can go fuck themselves. I'm going to take Sonia away from him. We'll leave Toronto. Go to Montreal maybe, I've cousins there. Or the States. The hell with this genteel jungle. Who needs a bloody law degree! I can always make a living in construction. Like my Papa. I was brought up on a building site. As soon as she gets her divorce from that creep, we'll get married, live decently, raise kids—" Weller interrupted.

"What about that million bucks? Sonia's a millionaire, you know. You planning to give it away?"

"Damn that million! I don't care!"

"Well, I care. What about me? Sure Sedgwick is a shit. But what choice do I have? He's my only chance. I've got a wife, two kids, one in college. And debts. I can't just go away, start a new life. And neither can you. Wise up, Ben. How do you know Sonia will go with you to be the wife of a construction worker? All this romantic bullshit. We have to stay and work it out. Both of us. There must be a way of getting at Sedgwick." Weller stopped and forced himself to focus on me. "What do you think, Helen? You're a smart girl."

"What did you tell the cops?" I asked.

"Not much. Just all I know. That's not all that much. But they're interested in Sedgwick, that's for sure. So maybe they'll pin something on him. Who knows?"

"And what will that do for you? If he goes down, so do you."

"Not necessarily. I didn't draw up that contract you know. Sedgwick did it all himself."

"What about the contract?"

"With Universal Sound. Or so it says. But it's really with him. When Sonia signs it, she'll belong to him."

"I'll murder the bastard, so help me!" Bono was beside himself. I put a hand on his arm and tried to calm him down. This was getting interesting.

"Tell me more. About the contract," I urged Weller.

"Nothing to tell. Sedgwick made a deal with Universal Sound. Under the table. They make Sonia a good-looking offer which ties her down plenty and then turn the contract over to Sedgwick. Another trophy for his collection. She won't be able to do a thing without his say so. Universal Sound is well covered; they can't lose. They are just making a deal with Sedgwick, doing him a favour. So he gets Sonia on a plate. Neat, eh?"

"You told the cops that?" I asked Weller. Bono was silent.

"Yeah, very carefully. Only what can be proved, what they could check. Sedgwick's a bad enemy to make. And I don't need enemies."

"Why did you tell them? You could've kept your mouth shut."

"That's what Sedgwick told me. 'Keep your mouth shut or else.' But even a worm will turn, you know."

"Uh," I said, unbelieving. Weller ignored me. He turned to Bono again.

"So you see Ben, we must stick together. Together we can destroy Sedgwick. And Sonia will be grateful. To both of us. She's going to pay that bomber to leave her alone; why not pay us?"

It was a significant argument for Weller to be making. Comparing his position to that of the 'bomber'. I sighed. Weller was a rat; a dirty, desperate rather dumb rat. He thought he needed Ben Bono to turn the tables on Sedgwick, to take some of the heat and to work on Sonia. Weller didn't want any romantic elopement which would leave him to face Sedgwick's 'or else' all alone. Suddenly my sense of urgency returned.

"Where's Karl Deerfield?" I asked. It must have sounded like a diversion. Weller didn't answer, back inside himself, pulling on his drink, staring into space, perhaps thinking of that million dollars. Bono answered:

"I don't know but when I went back to the hospital with Betty, he was there. Sonia wouldn't see him; Lew was with her. So Deerfield muttered something about going to talk to Walter and he left."

"Did he really think that Walt could persuade Sonia to see him? Why would Walt help him after what happened at Tri-Met?" It was my turn to sound surprised.

"Karl's big on the family bit. Still sees Walt as Sonia's husband and therefore the right person to talk to about Sonia. He's nuts. But he's her uncle."

"Thanks," I said. "Well, keep at it, boys. When you decide Sonia's future for her, let us all know." I couldn't help that piece of cheap sarcasm. But they both missed it, back in their several dreams of love and money.

I worked my way down past the busy bar, tables crowded with a mostly male clientele loudly getting smashed out of their gourds. The wide street outside was also busy with traffic. Maple Leaf Stadium had just emptied, hockey fans were streaming home and into bars to celebrate or mourn. If they were Leaf fans, then likely mourn.

Sonia's hotel, where my toothbrush rested, was just a block or two away. I wanted to rest too but couldn't. There were no cabs to be had so I walked to the subway, fighting the throng. I changed at Bloor Street and went west, getting off at the St. George station. From there it was just a short walk to Walt Lauker's place along the familiar street where I had sat in my late, lamented vehicle just three nights ago. The house was dark. I stood outside for a minute, remembering. Last time I had rushed in, gun in hand, fearful of what I might find. Tonight I had no gun and didn't feel like rushing in. My instinct had been wrong then, probably wrong again this time.

Again I tried to account for the feeling of urgency which had driven me all evening and which had brought me here. But it was no good. Slowly, reluctantly, quietly I tried the front door, pushed the bell of apartment #1. Silence. I fished out what passed for a 'manicure kit', my damaged hand clumsy. Under my somewhat rusty ministrations—I hadn't had occasion to pick a lock for a while—the door opened with a sharp click. The lobby was empty; I stepped over third class mail scattered on the floor and walked to Walt's apartment door. It was open an inch or so. I took a deep breath and went in.

For a moment I stood accustoming my eyes to the low light. A thin stream of light pushing its way out of the bathroom into the pitch dark room provided the only illumination. Slowly the bizarre collection of furniture and junk, valuables and garbage established themselves on my retina. A tall grandfather clock ticked distractingly in the background. With a rustle a small grey shape trotted towards me mewing. The cat ran past my legs out into the empty lobby. I shut the door behind me and looked around for the light switch. Couldn't find it. Turning again to the room which seemed suspended around me, something I had missed at first glance now registered. On the unmade bed where Walt had sat on my last visit here, a bundle of old clothing lay in a heap. Moving towards it quickly, I tripped over a knot of extension cords festooning the stacks of furniture and snaking their way across my path like the mesh of a trap. Cursing nervously under my breath I reached for the switch on the bed lamp. The bundle came into focus. It was Karl Deerfield. Or rather his body. It lay across the bed, hands clenched and face bloody. The head was smashed in, yet the pose looked comfortably relaxed. I looked down at all that was left of my prime suspect, my mind in an uproar. Murder. My sense of urgency had been well justified although the reason for it was as murky as ever.

Strangely, I felt relief. It's always easier to cope with the real thing, no matter how grisly, than wait for the unknown to happen. Turning away to go over the room, I noticed again the light streaming through the partly open bathroom door. My stomach rumbled inappropriately. I hadn't eaten all day, I realized suddenly. It's weird, the thoughts that crowd your head at times like these.

Shaking them off, in one step I was in the brightly lit bathroom. Unlike the room I had left it was modern, clean and uncluttered. Functional. The unexpected sterility made the sight of Walter Lauker's prone body sprawled on the shiny floor even more shocking. It took me a second to take in the whole scene. Bending down, I looked at his face and checked his pulse. He was alive, an almost empty gin bottle clasped to his chest. Not a foot away lay a rusty iron object of indeterminate use. It was stained dark with dried blood, bits of hair and scalp adhering to the rough surface. The murder weapon. The picture was dazzlingly clear to any child. Lauker had killed Deerfield in a fit of drunken rage and then passed out. So it seemed. Slowly I made my way to the phone and called Malory. It was going to be a long night.

22

Six hours later I was still there. In the interim, a police murder investigation took over, as formalized as classical ballet. The place became inundated with cops. At one point I counted seven police vehicles, five of them yellow, parked outside. At least a dozen uniformed officers, mostly young and crew-cut, wandered about asking questions and making important noises at neighbours and assorted rubber-neckers. Plainclothes detectives moved officiously in and out, muttering at each other, to Malory, to the coroner's crew. They took photographs, measurements, peered under furniture, searched every nook and cranny of the crowded murder room.

Deerfield's body had finally been removed and Walt Lauker taken away in an ambulance under police escort. Superintendent Sterling, there in person, was on the phone talking to departmental powers-that-be.

I sat, licking my Swiss Chalet dinner which I had managed to have delivered, off my fingers. Sergeant Malory sat across from me trying hard not to look overly pleased. I could understand what it was that had made his day. Of itself the murder of an obscure Owen Sound nut case was small potatoes. Solving it had involved no work, and cops are bureaucrats and don't like difficult cases and extra work any more than anyone else. The reason to celebrate was that through this murder they appeared to have disposed of a politically heavy bombing. That their perpetrator was Walter Lauker was pure gravy.

"Well, I guess we can wrap it up for the night. Tomorrow we'll start back-tracking, tying Lauker and Deerfield to the bombing, and to Miss Deerfield's other troubles. Won't be difficult," Malory said happily. "As soon as these connections are established we'll have a solid case against Lauker. Copperplated. Are you satisfied? I can let you leave Toronto in a week or so. Of course you'll have to be back for the trial. But that's months away."

"Good of you. But I'm not satisfied, as well you know."

"Too bad. I don't see why not. Karl Deerfield was the prowler you almost caught, yes or no? You can't get away from the evidence. He had a room at the Imperial Palace Hotel. You yourself found that out, I give you credit. He'd been one of the hotel regulars ever since the lottery win. That's when the various incidents started. So what more do you want?"

"Why did Lauker kill him?" I asked.

"Any number of possible motives. Someone else had to be in this with Deerfield, you agree? Lauker had been the chief suspect all along. He and Deerfield got together to scare Miss Deerfield into passing her win on to her uncle. What could be more natural? I read this murder as a falling-out between partners in crime. Happens all the time. Deerfield probably set the bomb. Then came here to see his partner. Perhaps they quarrelled. Anyway, Lauker killed him. He was dead less than an hour when you called us, who else could've done it? Except you, that is." Malory smiled when he said that.

Malory's explanation made sense only to someone who didn't know Sonia's family history with Uncle Karl. He was the last person on earth she would ever trust. Lauker knew that. Which destroyed his motive. Why would he get involved with Karl Deerfield? Of course, Malory didn't know any of this; I hadn't told him. Under these circumstances all I could do was to withdraw gracefully. Which wasn't easy.

"Yeah, yeah. Happy days. Can I go now?" I said.

"Sure. We'll need you in the morning."

Sterling hung up and joined us as Malory finished speaking.

"Miss Keremos, we'll be charging Walter Lauker with first degree murder tomorrow. And making a statement to the press. I was just talking to the Chief and the Assistant Crown Prosecutor. It's been agreed. There will be formal depositions from you and the others in this case. It would be advisable that you confine yourself to the facts and not attempt to confuse the issue with any unfounded suspicions. Be assured that all aspects are being properly investigated."

"Unfounded suspicions! Who decides what's unfounded? What you really mean is that I should keep my mouth shut and not let the press in on what I know."

"What you believe you know. Yes. As I said, there will be a public statement issued, probably a formal press briefing. Then the matter is *sub judice* and any comments constitute contempt of court. I suggest you govern yourself accordingly."

"Nicely put. OK. I don't have much choice so I won't contradict the official version. But I still have a client and as far as I'm concerned the case isn't over. Good night."

I yawned, and walked out of the strangely familiar gruesome apartment. As I got out of earshot I saw Sterling turn to Malory. Instructions. I guessed I would be having police company for the next few days. It figured.

23

NEXT DAY WAS HECTIC. I barely had time to talk to Sonia over an obviously tapped phone. Our authorities love tapping phones and Canadians put up with much more of this kind of invasion of privacy than do Americans. Anyway they found out what they already knew. That Sonia had gotten the very best criminal lawyer for Lauker. I got instructions to talk to him, to brief him, to help him in any way possible to defend Lauker. Also she was leaving the hospital and moving back into her own place.

That was good news. We were much more likely to have privacy there and that was important. I needed to talk to her; I needed time; I needed to get things clear in my head; I needed to contact the rest of the crew; I needed to know whether the cops were serious in tying Lauker and Deerfield together to the harassment and the bombing; I needed sleep. I needed to be triplets. But I wasn't. I was one tired and bruised forty-year-old woman.

I asked Sonia if Betty was still with her. It turned out that she'd just left, having spent the night at the hospital in the empty bed beside Sonia's. My bed of the day before. There'd been lots of palaver about her staying there. Hospital authorities can be more inflexible and red-tape-ridden than any civil servant. Finally a bright Night Sister had closed her eyes to Betty's presence and allowed her to spend the night at Sonia's side. Now Betty had left to make her statement to the police. My first task was to track her down.

I found Betty Grelick just leaving Police Headquarters when I got there to do my act for the benefit of the stenographers. We stopped and chatted. She agreed to wait for me a few blocks away at the Ritz Tearoom. Immediately I called Alex and asked her to join us. She would have sufficient time to get there from the Beaches, I reckoned.

My formal deposition was a joke. They wanted as little from

me as possible. That way if in the future I brought up anything else, I could be discredited for not having included it in my original statement. There is only so much credibility attached to claiming, "But I wasn't asked!" The Crown knew or guessed that I would be one of the defence witnesses. It made sense to discredit me in advance. Our system of criminal jurisprudence functions on the basis of which side can best bamboozle the judge and jury. Truth and justice have little to do with it.

I wasn't overly concerned. Walter Lauker might be a poor weirdo in the eyes of the law but he was getting the best defence money could buy. The prosecution would have to be careful. Crown couldn't get away with anything really gross. If it ever came to trial, that is. Malory's scenario still didn't ring true to me.

Coming out of the dull red brick police building I was hailed by Malory. He hadn't been present at my statement-making, that chore having been delegated to a junior sergeant.

"Well," he said.

"Well, what?" I answered.

"We have the goods on Lauker, you know. Deerfield was definitely responsible for the explosion. We found dynamite and detonators in his room at the Imperial. Can you imagine! And those 'incidents' and phone calls to his niece. He must've gotten his information through Lauker. We figure it for a plot between Lauker and Deerfield to force Sonia into allowing Karl to handle her lottery money. Then the two of them would split whatever they could get their hands on and blame it on some outsider."

"Really. And what does Walt say to all that?"

"Nothing. He isn't talking so far. Bail hearing has been set. He'll plead innocent and hope to get off on a technicality. With the heavy-weight defence he's got in his corner, he just might do it, too."

"Another miscarriage of justice, eh? Cops work their pinkies to the bone to preserve law and order and stupid courts let the bad guys go 'on a technicality'. Come on, Malory. You know damn well something smells about this Deerfield/Lauker set-up. You've taken the easy way out. Don't you want to know what really happened?"

Malory shrugged and prepared to move off.

"Just don't make waves," he said. Then something occurred to him. "Are you still after Sedgwick? I hope not, for your sake."

"After him for murder you mean? No."

"For anything." He was frowning at me. I got impatient.

"Oh, Malory, for Christ sake! The man's an egomaniac with as many human scruples as a crocodile."

"It's not against the law to be an egomaniac. There's nothing on him. Leave it alone." Malory was angry. I'd hit a nerve.

"Maybe, maybe not. I guess crooked contracts and under-the-table payoffs are par for the course these days. Or are you saying, you're homicide, it's not your bailiwick? All right, I understand. But don't give me any shit, there's plenty on him. All it needs is some gumption and a little work. If Weller and some gink at Universal could be made to testify, we could cut Sedgwick down. How about it?"

Malory let his breath out slowly.

"So you know about the contract. I was afraid you might. OK. I'll make you a deal. Get the goods on Sedgwick on that and I'll go along. But it better be good. Otherwise no one will touch it. Certainly not the Law Society. When was a man of Sedgwick's stature last disbarred in this province? Tell me that! It's not worth my time going after someone like Sedgwick unless there is more than enough evidence for criminal action. And that'll be the day!"

Malory's reaction was natural. He would love to get Sedgwick. There's no love lost between cops and high-priced, big-shit lawyers. If he could trip up Sedgwick with no risk to himself, he would. But he wasn't about to take a chance and endanger his job. I'd have to do the work for him.

"How's about a nice juicy civil suit against Sedgwick? All over the papers. Criminal charges could wait if and when we turn up enough dirt. And we will, count on it. Will you play?"

"Sure. That's different. No skin off my ass."

"Then give me what you've got so far. You got something

from Weller, I know. Names, dates, numbers. I'll take it from there."

He looked at me doubtfully.

"I'll think about it. You are persistent, aren't you? You also going to try to queer this Lauker thing for us?"

"Believe it."

"Then how about a swap. You leave Lauker to me and I'll give you what I've on Sedgwick. Do we have a deal?"

I laughed and shook my head.

He said, "I didn't think so. Well, let's leave it at that for now. If you change your mind, let me know."

"Likewise. Yeah, let's leave it. Amazing how things change. Make you a small wager. Within forty-eight hours, maybe twenty-four, Lauker will be out, the case will have changed and you'll wish you'd listened to me. Do we have a bet?"

"I'm not a betting man."

"You're betting this case is going to turn out the way you see it now. I should make Sterling the same offer. I bet he hedges his bets."

Malory wasn't amused.

"I wouldn't approach Sterling if I were you. I'm telling you Helen, leave it alone!"

I noted the obvious pleading, the man-to-man treatment he was handing me. Not a tactic which works, as Malory should have known by now. So I just smiled. We parted relatively amicably.

It was a short walk to the Ritz Tearoom in the basement of an old house just off Yonge Street. The place is small; more than twenty people make it a crowd. Alex hadn't arrived yet. I ordered coffee, a salad and a muffin and sat down next to Betty Grelick at one of the tiny tables we shared with another couple. Not a place for confidences.

Betty looked haggard. She wasn't as trendy-spruce as usual. Misapplied eyeshadow covered the dark hollows under her eyes. I wondered idly why she bothered. Habit probably, self-protection. Unfortunately all it did was make her look older, tired and unable to cope. She stirred her tea mechanically and without looking at me said, "Isn't it terrible about Walt? And Uncle Karl, of course. The police came and questioned Sonia this morning. She was very upset. Naturally."

"Naturally," I repeated. She took it as a comment.

"Well, they were her husband and her uncle, you know."

"When I talked with her she was much more upset by Walt's arrest than by Karl's death. Have you noticed that?"

"Yes, that does seem strange. But Sonia has always been very fond of Walt. And she never stopped. She just didn't want to be married to him any more. People can't understand that but it makes sense to me."

At the mention of 'arrest' and 'death' our two table mates fell silent, finding our conversation more interesting than their own. I ignored them, swallowed a bite of salad and said, "Sure. Doesn't mean you hate a guy just because you don't want to be lovers or married to him. Or to anyone else. But did Walt understand that? Few men do."

"I think he understood. He wasn't happy she left him but knew it was inevitable, really. Now she'll do all she can to get him off this charge. Even though he's supposed to have been plotting against her with her uncle. That's another thing people don't understand."

"What's this about people not understanding? Who? What people? Why does it matter?"

"It doesn't I guess. Yet—it's difficult to do things that make people disapprove of you. Sonia can do it, I can't."

Betty looked at me, her tired eyes grave. The two eaves-droppers held their breath. She continued, "I don't have a family. Not any; I was brought up in group homes and by foster parents. So I know how important people's approval can be. How you have to behave to be accepted. Everyone had power over me. The child care workers, the police, the courts, the staff at the group home, foster parents, teachers. Even other kids. That's what made me the way I am. Perhaps if I hadn't been an orphan—"

"Sonia wasn't an orphan. Her family sure didn't do much for her. She made her own way, didn't she?"

"So did I, so did I."

"You both did OK as these things go. So what does it all prove?"

I must have looked my impatience. Betty shrugged.

"All right, you've made your point, whatever it is. We both did OK. Now Sonia is in hospital, her uncle is dead and her husband is under arrest for murder. And I don't know whether I'm coming or going; or what I feel or think about it all. So what's your advice, smartass?"

"What's this with advice? You don't need advice. Neither does Sonia. And you shouldn't take it if you get it. Hey, here's Alex."

Alex stalked in, looked around, pounced on an empty table and motioned us to join her. Which Betty and I did, to the great disappointment of our eavesdroppers. Betty and Alex had met previously at the hospital and seemed to have hit it off. It was a good opportunity to get some matters sorted out. We started by going over Betty's knowledge of the events of the previous evening. Alex listened carefully. We were trying to establish Karl Deerfield's itinerary. Who knew that he'd intended to go to Walt Lauker's place?

"We all did. Ben and Lew, Sonia and I. We were all there in her hospital room at the same time and Sedgwick was just leaving so he might have heard it also. But Karl couldn't have gone straight to Walt's from there, could he? Not if he was your prowler in the apartment," Betty explained.

"That's right. He must've gone from the hospital to the hotel. The time fits. Then on to Walt's. Hm. What were the others doing during that time?"

"No idea. Ben Bono left to get Chuck Weller out of custody. Lew just took off, he didn't say where he was going."

"What did you all talk about?"

"Various things. The explosion, of course. Whether the bomber and extortionist were one and the same. And whether Sonia should offer to pay up as she was proposing to do. Someone wondered whether you had put her up to it. Did you?"

"It's probably all academic now. There won't be any more phone calls or demands."

"You mean now that Karl Deerfield is dead, murdered by his accomplice, there isn't anyone to do it? But if it wasn't Walter then why wouldn't the real accomplice continue harassment?" Betty was being unnecessarily obtuse, it seemed to me.

"Either Walter did it or he is being set up by someone. Any further extortion demands would indicate that Walter wasn't Karl's accomplice or at least that a third party is involved. As it is, the cops are ready to close the case. They think they've got everyone concerned in this, the callers, the bomber and the murderer. It's smart to let them continue to believe that."

Betty didn't look satisfied. She might have objected but Alex chimed in, "Hey, if you want to get Walter Lauker off the hook, how about making an extortion demand? That would confuse the cops, maybe—" Alex stopped, looked at us and added hurriedly, "OK, OK, it's just a thought. Forget it."

"I wouldn't dignify it by calling it a thought. Look. There can't be any more extortion calls. Karl Deerfield was responsible for them. For anyone else to try it now would be madness. That particular game is over."

Alex winked at Betty, trying to lighten the atmosphere, and said, "Watch the Great Detective at work. Now in words of one syllable tell us about Karl Deerfield and his mysterious partner."

"OK. Karl Deerfield and the unknown Mr. or Ms X decided to shake down Sonia. I bet Karl made the calls, was fed information by X who was on the inside in Sonia's inner circle."

"One of us," said Betty. It wasn't a question.

"Had to be. The purse-snatching or the almost-accident or both could've been coincidences. The conspirators took advantage of these incidents by claiming responsibility. Once you can establish yourself as a threat plus have inside knowledge, it's dead easy. You can take credit for and magnify every little thing that happens. Generate fear with no risk to yourself."

"What about the break-in?"

"My guess is, Karl was responsible for that. What we don't know is if that was his private initiative or part of a plan agreed upon with his partner. Either way, it precipitated matters. Even Sedgwick couldn't keep a lid on it after that. So I was hired. That freaked out Deerfield, although he tried to cover it up at first. Anyway, he went bananas and put that bomb in my truck. To get rid of me. Remember his background. In Army Engineers and later with highways. He had knowledge and access to explosives. Now at this point the whole plot was way out of hand. His partner got badly scared that this old man had lost his marbles, endangering both of them. Deerfield had to die, and so was murdered. A fall guy had to be provided to take the murder rap. Very tidy. Case closed."

"Very tidy. Now what?"

"Your guess is as good as mine. Let's go over the possibilities. As long as the frame on Lauker holds or appears to hold, the real murderer would be smart to lie low. Do nothing. Let things take their course. As long as everything is concentrated on Lauker, he's safe. But if the frame doesn't stay tight, then all bets are off."

"What d'you mean, 'all bets are off'?" Betty inquired anxiously.

"I mean that anything is possible."

"You mean you don't know." That was Alex, of course. What are friends for.

"Yep. That's what I mean. Any more questions?"

"Not if your answers are as illuminating as that."

Alex leaned back and lit a cigarette. At least three people in our vicinity looked accusingly at her. Betty was getting restless.

"I have to go help Sonia out of hospital. She shouldn't be going yet but she insists. She'll be worried if I don't show up on time. Take care."

"You too. Alex and I'll meet you at the apartment. 'Bye," I said. We watched Betty leave the restaurant. Alex gave a sigh, of relief I think.

"Uph! That's a heavy lady. What's her problem?" she said.

"I don't know what her therapist would say, but my guess

is that she's come up against a major barrier in her life and doesn't know what to do about it. She's gotten along so far just trying to make it up from under, not be poor and a nobody. Now that's more or less accomplished she doesn't know what comes next."

"You also mean she doesn't realize that she's in love with Sonia." Not much gets past Alex.

"Yeah. And if she did it would only scare her shitless. So let's drop it. As Nate says, 'everyone's in love with Sonia'. Except Sonia," I answered.

We dropped the subject.

"Alex, let's concentrate on the next step. You go on to the apartment and keep an eye on Sonia. I've a couple of things to check out."

"Like what for instance?"

"The situation calls for a discussion with Lew Davies. Don't you agree?"

"Because Betty thinks Lew did it; yes, I agree."

"I love it when you get the smarts. There's no one like you then. Yes, Betty makes Lew as Karl's accomplice. She's scared that he'll continue to try to get his hands on Sonia's money. That's why I told her it wouldn't happen after you set it up so nicely."

"You think she bought it? Seemed pretty obvious to me that you were warning her off."

"You know me. She doesn't. Anyway she's not thinking too clearly. So my next move is to be Lew Davies."

"Then what?"

"Depends. Perhaps Sedgwick," I replied.

"I wouldn't want you as an enemy. You're still after him, eh? Heavier and heavier. Look at you. Bruises all over, a bum arm and you go on like Superwoman."

"Nuts. I'm OK. What d'you want me to do, retire?"

We both laughed. Alex gave me a hug, carefully avoiding my 'bum arm'. It hurt all the same but it was worth it. I left her feeling almost up to what I was planning to do. Almost.

24

I WALKED DOWN YONGE STREET. A careful lookout for cars which hung back blocking traffic established a green Dodge Dart with two men in it. My tail, courtesy Metropolitan Toronto Police Department. At Wellesley I sprinted into the subway entrance and down the stairs to the south-bound platform. No luck. A train had just pulled out and one of the men from the car had plenty of time to follow, spot me and take position near the exit in case I changed my mind about taking the south-bound train. The car would have stopped (illegally) where the driver could watch the exits to street and buses. So far, all was according to standard procedure.

The south-bound train along Yonge Street makes a turn at Union Station and starts north again under the dull splendour of University Avenue. I sat still, staring blankly at the advertisements on the car walls, glad of a rest. At College I was on my feet making unnecessarily early preparations to get off at the next stop, Museum. My tail, on the look out for misdirection, was in no hurry to leave the platform. He had seen enough movies to know that the best way to avoid being followed on the subway was to jump back onto the train just as the doors close. I was sorry to disappoint him. His clever delay did cost him that extra ten seconds which gave me time to get across Bloor Street and be heading east by the time he emerged. I was quite visible and in no apparent hurry so he could relax and mutter some incantation into his walkie-talkie. I wondered how this new breed of plain-clothes cop would fare without all those expensive wonders-of-modern-technology at their disposal. As it happens, I didn't care about this young cop's ability to communicate with his partner but I was counting on his habitual reliance on cars for transportation.

He had paid in cash at Wellesley. Chances were, he didn't have any subway tokens good at turnstiles. I walked purposefully along Bloor, turned sharply left down an alley and thirty seconds later pushed a subway token into an automatic gate at an unattended entrance. Without a token my tail would have to go to the regular entrance a block away. I sprinted down to the east-bound platform and was lucky to get a train within seconds. At rest again, I visualized my pursuer huffing and puffing into the mike, making excuses for losing me. My victory over the forces which claim to serve and protect us was small but sweet. It allowed me to forget my aches and pains until at Castle Frank station I grabbed a south-bound bus. Getting off in Cabbagetown I walked into the maze of small one-way streets. My one and only visit to Davies' place had been by car with Sonia navigating. I took my time, orienting myself, carefully zigging and zagging just in case. There was no point in taking the trouble to throw off a tail only to be picked up by some watchful detective right on Lew Davies' doorstep.

A block short of his house I turned and walked along the street which paralleled his, looking for the house which backed onto his yard. It turned out to be one of those tarted up townhouses; sand blasted, beshuttered, wrought ironed, brass lamp lit and overrun with stained glass windows and sky lights, all on a seventeen-foot frontage. Two stone dogs dressed in enormous iron chains guarded the dinky front door. Glory be.

Nothing and nobody guarded the way into the alley between the two streets. It was close to six. People just getting home from work. People having their first pre-dinner drink. It was dead easy not to be spotted. I scrambled painfully over the back fence into Davies' yard. No sign of the cops. The back door didn't take me a second.

I was in his kitchen. There were bottles of gin, of tonic, a half-empty ice cube tray on the counter. Pleasant sounds of ice in a glass drifted in from the next room along with the TV news. Lew Davies was in the livingroom, glass in hand, watching TV. Softly I poured myself a gin and tonic and walked into the large room to join him. He jerked round suddenly and stared. Letting out a loud breath, he got heavily to his feet, still holding onto the glass. I saluted him with mine, and said, "Mind if I join you?"

"Mind—?! What the hell is this? Where did you come from? What do you want?"

"One question at a time, please. I came through the back so as not to disturb Metro's finest in case they are watching you. Are they?"

"The cops? No. Why should they?"

"Why indeed. No call at all. Good. We can make ourselves comfortable." I sat down and sipped my drink. The TV blared on. CBC's News Hour at six o'clock. I stretched my legs and watched. Davies was still standing, disconcerted.

"All right," he said, punched the box to turn off the TV and sat down. "What d'you want from me this time? What more is there? The case is closed, or haven't you heard."

"Right. Now that Karl Deerfield is dead you've nothing to worry about, do you?"

"Now that Karl is dead and Walt arrested it's all over. Well, isn't it? Now Sonia can pay you whatever exorbitant fee you'll demand from her and the rest of us can go back to our lives again in peace." He said it with calm conviction. He was good.

"If Walt killed Karl," I stated just as calmly.

"What are you on about! Of course he did. They caught him, didn't they?"

"He was found drunk on the bathroom floor. Conveniently passed out with the murder weapon beside him."

Lew Davies looked at me again more carefully over the rim of his glass. He shrugged and said, "Look, you may believe what you like but it seems simple to me. Walt and Karl have been trying to scare Sonia into turning those dollars over to Uncle Karl, at least temporarily. He's been after her about it for months. Wanting to look after her and her interests, of course. And the police have evidence he placed that bomb and vandalized her apartment. To scare her. What more does anyone need?"

"Amazing how reasonable it sounds. But evidence against

Karl as the 'mad bomber', prowler and phone freak is not proof that Walt was his accomplice or his murderer. If it wasn't Walter Lauker, who was it? What are the possibilities? Sedgwick—it was dead against his interest to draw attention to the fact that Sonia was independently wealthy. And would he want to have Karl on his hands? No way. Weller—a possibility from a motive standpoint but means and opportunity are pretty iffy. He wasn't his own man, Sedgwick is boss. I doubt there is much he doesn't know about Weller. Bono—Ben Bono is out. He's a romantic, conventional young male in love with Sonia. A plot like this is totally outside his scope or comprehension. He doesn't need Sonia's money. I bet he would insist on 'keeping her' on his own salary if they ever got married. Who does that leave?" I paused, watching Davies watching me. He looked away as if for means of escape. Perhaps it was just my imagination.

"That leaves Betty and me. Well, how about Betty?" he said bravely.

"Yes, how about Betty? Would you like to make a case against her? Betty is the only one of you all with an alibi! Think about that. She was in the hospital continuously from before Karl left there until his body was found, by me. That leaves you."

Tension in the room went up a couple of notches. The room was silent and still. Finally Lew Davies spoke.

"It's Walt. They will stick with Walt. He was there; why should they drop him to go after me?"

"What 'they'? You mean the cops. Yes, they like Walt Lauker as the murderer. But Sonia is sure that Walt would never be in any plot against her with Uncle Karl. It's pretty clear that she will come to the conclusion that it was you as soon as she has time to think. Then, regardless of what happens about Lauker, you will lose her." As I spoke Lew Davies became more and more agitated. Reference to Sonia did that to him.

"I must talk to Sonia. I must make her understand—"

A loud phone ring interrupted him. Putting down his drink impatiently, Davies picked up the receiver.

"Hello, Lew Davies here." His melodic Welsh lilt became

more pronounced. "Oh, hi, Betty." He listened in silence for a couple of minutes. Then, "She's here. You should talk to her." Without a word he handed me the receiver and walked out of the room.

"Helen, Helen, listen." Betty was breathless. "I was just telling Lew. Walt is out. He's coming here—"

"Where?" I inquired. I heard a click and Sonia's voice cut in.

"Helen, you did it! They're letting Walt go! He's coming here to the apartment to tell us all what happened. He insisted. Wouldn't talk at the police station, the cops have to come here to hear him. But he won't talk to them directly, only in front of me and us all. Oh, isn't that great!"

"We're on our way," I said. As I put the receiver down Lew Davies appeared wearing a jacket.

"Let's go," he said. We went out back to Sonia's white Volvo.

The drive was short. Neither of us spoke, deep in our respective thoughts.

We went up in the elevator and down the long corridor to Sonia's apartment. Inside, arranged like a tableau, were the three women, Sonia, Betty, and Alex Edwards. As we entered I noted Alex signaling me frantically. Betty was pouring herself a drink. Sonia smiled at us from the depth of her armchair. Lew went up to her, grabbed her hand and kissed it.

"How are you, my dear." He would have continued in this vein but it was obvious he didn't have Sonia's attention. She spoke at me.

"And what do you think, Helen! There's been an extortion demand. Yes, sometime yesterday someone called the answering service. Today when I arrived here and collected my calls, there it was. Alex, what did it say?"

Betty burst in before Alex could answer.

"You said there wouldn't be an extortion demand—"

"Never mind about that now," I interrupted. "What's the demand say and when did it arrive? Alex!"

"Seems nobody bothered to check with the answering service since Sonia's been in hospital. So when we got back here today there was a whole bunch of messages. Mostly get-well sort of stuff. Among them was one dated yesterday afternoon which said—I took this over the phone, you understand, but I made sure they gave me everything that was on the original message slip—which said: 'Two hundred thousand is the number. Get it together. Place and time to follow.' That's all. No source, no name, no signature. It was a man's voice. That's all anyone knows. What do you think? Is that a demand or is that a demand?"

"No shit. All right, Sonia are you getting it together?" I asked Sonia. She nodded lightly.

"Tomorrow morning when the trust company opens they will have the money ready. I hope they don't tell the cops."

"So do I. Well, isn't that fascinating."

"I told Malory about Uncle Karl. I told him that I would testify that Walt knew I would never, under any circumstances, let Karl handle my money," Sonia continued.

"Yes," I commented slowly.

"If that was the basis of the plot then Walt is out of it."

"But this demand doesn't fit," Lew broke in. "It's got nothing to do with Karl Deerfield. It's just plain extortion. Walt could've killed Deerfield and an accomplice as well."

Sonia would have none of it. She said, "Drop it for now, all of you. Let's hear Walt's story. He'll be here soon. With Malory and Sterling."

"Well, Walt'll have himself a great audience. God, how he must be loving this. Cops' noses out of joint and everyone just hanging on his every word."

"Now, Helen, let's not be petty. Walt's had a bad time. He deserves a little of what he fancies from his friends. As long as nobody else suffers, that's all I ask."

The conversation moved back and forth, Alex contributing her share. We were putting in time until Walt's arrival. That guy couldn't pass up an opportunity to make a dramatic entrance. Had to hand it to him, though. He was no small-time poseur. Under the circumstances, holding out from the cops took a lot of guts. But guts or no guts Walter Lauker was a pain.

25

"No more chains, no more dungeons!" Walt Lauker was doing his act for our benefit. Especially for Sonia's. She was smiling indulgently at his small boy antics.

I glanced at Malory, hoping to get a chance to talk to him privately but he wasn't interested. He watched Walt sourly. Unsurprisingly, he was not amused at Walt's elaborate and highly imaginative tale of his 'incarceration', as Walt insisted on calling his overnight detention. Undoubtedly Walt had been under some considerable and unpleasant pressure by the police to make a statement. Preferably a damaging one, of course. He had withstood the stress and opted to stand mute until this dramatic performance could be arranged.

"Thumbscrews, 'twas to be thumbscrews, next." Walt presented his undamaged thumbs for our inspection. The power of his acting made every one of us look at them, as if expecting to see them mangled out of recognition. Watching our reaction to his story, Walt grinned with satisfaction.

"But I held out and justice triumphed. So here I am free and at your feet, my gorgeous Sonia!"

"Walter, you great idiot! Calm down now. Yes, sure it's good to see you free and in good shape. You've Helen to thank for that, you know. She bugged the police into letting you go." Malory cleared his throat. Sonia glanced at him then went on, ignoring his wordless protest. "Now you must tell us what happened. No more silly games. Without your evidence about the night Karl got killed the police are helpless." This time Malory sounded like the last trump.

"Something wrong with your throat, Sergeant?" inquired Walt, unfazed by Sonia's scolding. Putting his hands up to his mouth he yodelled:

"Calling Brothers Smith!" in a fair imitation of the old Philip Morris commercial.

"Stop it, stop it now, Walt. That's enough. You've gotten all the mileage you deserve out of this situation. I know, who better, that you can milk it for hours. But it's too serious for games."

Sonia's voice had an edge to it now. An edge that Walter Lauker obviously recognized. He started to wind himself down a bit. Not dropping his persona completely but at least becoming more coherent and to the point. Sprawled next to Sonia on the couch, his hand in hers, the centre of attention—he was having a ball. Modifying his performance to make a consecutive story, he launched into a dramatic description of the evening of Karl Deerfield's death.

"There I was, in my humble abode, having a late snack. Just me and my old pal Herod."

"That's his cat," explained Sonia.

"Yes. Please don't interrupt. In good time, all will be made clear to the meanest intelligence. Anyway, the two of us were half way through a can of delicious smoked oysters when who should present himself for our amusement but dear Uncle Karl. A little flurried and very indignant. His story was that he happened to be in this suite when he was viciously attacked and pursued by Helen, here present. What exactly his business was in your suite he didn't specify, but I suspect he was after your undies, Sonia, my sweet," Walt continued, carried away by his eloquence. At the look on Sonia's face he went on hurriedly.

"Well anyway, Herod and I welcomed him, providing him with a chair—not an easy task, you know, in my little home—and a proper manly drink. Rye, I think it was. Under the influence of our ministrations dear Uncle Karl waxed quite eloquent about his concern for Sonia, and how seriously he took his familial responsibilities. I'm sure it comes as a surprise to us all that he still thought of you as a little girl in need of his love and protection."

This was too much for Sonia.

"Stop it, Walt," she warned him.

"All right, I guess that's a bit raw," he conceded. "But most of it is necessary for Sergeant Malory's notebook. Please understand one and all, that Karl wasn't mad. He knew perfectly well that Sonia is a grown woman and he wasn't under any illusion as to how she felt about him. He certainly seemed to know what he was doing. Just didn't care, that's all. He was proud of his maneouvers around Sonia. In fact he regaled us with his exploits. The calls, the war of nerves, the vandalism, all that he freely admitted. More, he took credit for it. But he did have some difficulty telling Herod and me about how he engineered the bomb. That was aimed at Helen, of course. She was in his way."

Walter stopped for seconds, the better to gauge our reactions. Satisfied, he went on. "He'd no liking for me, that's for sure. But he saw me as his only hope after all that had transpired. The way he saw it, Sonia, you're surrounded by villains and illwishers. He was horrified by Helen, an obvious tough dyke. So I was to help him get you away from all that bad, bad influence. The first step towards this admirable end was for Uncle Karl to take charge as head-of-the-house. At your hotel suite, naturally. That would give him access to you. So he could protect you and your money. Hey, that was his story not mine!"

Walt took a deep breath. "Now I may not be the best and the brightest in this land but all this highfalutin' altruism was pretty hard to swallow. I indicated my honest doubts to dear uncle. Also, in my most beguiling manner I asked him who was in all this with him. I'm afraid he took my scepticism rather badly. I was supposed to be the idiot in-law. I was supposed to bow to his authority. 'I didn't come here to be interrogated,' he told me. It was merely my duty to cooperate. He was very unhappy. He'd gone through life with the conviction that anyone who's not pretty conventional is by definition stupid or nuts. Anyway, certainly of no account. First, Helen had kind of shaken that world view of his, since she was clearly someone very much to be taken seriously. Now I was being uppity. But it turned out that worst of all was Lew Davies' insubordination, as he finally described it. He and Lew had been playing tricks on Sonia together—those are Karl's words for it. But the scheme wasn't working as expected. Lew was to have been like a good NCO, but he'd refused to play his part. He refused an order. Horrors! Karl had done the bomb number without Lew's knowledge or permission and apparently Lew had taken umbrage. As well he might. So Karl had nowhere to turn. That's why he'd come to me with his absurd demand that I help him into Sonia's life. To cut a long story short, there we were happily consuming great quantities of rye and ginger when my old friend Lew Davies arrived."

At the first, earlier mention of his name, Lew Davies froze, only his eyes moving between Walt and Sonia. It appeared that his only concern was the effect Walt's story was having on her.

We were certainly getting to the nitty-gritty. Malory ostentatiously turned over a page in his notebook and rearranged his bulk in the chair. Sonia lay back and said nothing. Her face, framed by the halo of burnished hair, was grave, white, eyes almost unblinking. My heart went out to her.

"Yes, Lew arrived. Very jolly and friendly. 'Good old Walt, good old Karl!' Let's all have a drink, would I like a snort of coke? By the by Sergeant, you and your bird-dogs didn't find any cocaine on my premises and you never will. But that doesn't mean that I won't indulge in the heavenly stuff when it's offered. Lew was often very generous with it, you know. So he was friendly as hell that night. But also in a hurry. Mostly he wanted to get Karl out of there, to remove him so he wouldn't spill the beans. But Lew is a smart lad. It didn't take him long to figure out that it was too late. Karl had already unloaded to me."

Again that pause, pregnant with tension. Malory sighed. Walter's story was interesting but wasn't very useful as testimony. It was short on the concrete—when, who, where, how—and long on assumptions, interpretations and opinions. So it would all have to be gone over again at dictation speed according to the acceptable police procedure. A policeman's lot is not a happy one, I thought inconsequentially, but then who would choose to be a copper!

"So then Lew decided to tell me his side of the story. It seems that he was only helping Uncle Karl to his proper place at Sonia's side. Altruism again. So I laughed. My hilarity wasn't appreciated. At first Lew thought I was doubting the unselfishness of his motives but then I told him that Uncle Karl was absolutely the last person in the whole wide world that Sonia would allow near her under any circumstances. I didn't have to spell it out too much before Lew realized that he'd been conned out of his little blue socks by Karl, that old never-was. Naturally he was mad as hell. So he hit me, not very hard but hard enough. I was drunk by then anyway, so I passed out."

Walter stopped. He'd lost his audience. Everyone looked at Lew Davies, who was shaking his head in apparent disbelief.

"A fairy tale. My god, Walter, this is too much. Now you're going to claim that you saw me kill Karl!"

"No. Like I said, I passed out. When I came to I was in custody of Malory and his merry men. Maybe you didn't kill Karl. But then, who did? You were there."

Sonia looked stunned as the two men argued about which one of them killed Karl. Everyone else just sat there. It was quite a scene. Malory sighed again.

"Well, you didn't expect a witness to the actual murder, did you?" I said to him quietly.

"Would've been nice. It happens. Especially in homicides in the family. And that's most of them. Dangerous things, families." He turned from me and raised his voice addressing the three people most concerned.

"Please, Miss Deerfield, gentlemen. I think we've had enough. Mr. Davies, in the light of Mr. Lauker's story we'll want another statement from you. I expect you'll want to talk to a lawyer. Will you be getting a lawyer for him, Miss Deerfield?"

"Yes," Sonia said unequivocally.

"Yes, so he'll have the best defence. Oh, well, not my problem." Malory spoke as if Davies wasn't present. He stood up heavily, and tucked away his notebook. "And we'll need a formal statement of what you just told us, from you, Mr. Lauker. And Miss Deerfield, a full description of your childhood relationship with the victim. Sorry, but it's necessary. Including Mr. Lauker's prior knowledge of your feelings about your uncle. You understand that is required to remove any possibility of a rational motive on the part of your husband." He stressed the 'rational', significantly.

Sergeant Francis Malory of Metropolitan Toronto Police was no dumb flatfoot to be taken lightly or made a fool of. I suspected that Walter Lauker was in for some very unpleasant time, whether he was guilty of any major crime or not.

It didn't help that Malory wasn't happy with the case against Davies, so far. For that matter, neither was I. As it stood it was Lauker's word against his. It would need a hell of a lot more than that to convict. So Malory's manner was understandable. He was playing it cool, hoping to force Davies' hand, make him do something dumb. It worked. Unable to stand the pervasive, low-level tension, unable to understand what was happening, Davies burst out, addressing himself to Sonia.

"No! No! Please understand. It wasn't like that. I didn't mean—"

As the words left his mouth, I moved towards him. Davies recollected himself, his body swung around, his arms shot out to push me out of his way. I sprawled on the floor trying to get my feet under me. Before the three cops in the room could react, Lew Davies was out of there and pounding down the silent hotel corridor. Malory swore, Sterling looked around for a telephone, presumably to call reinforcements. Only the young cop took off after Davies, without wasting any time. By the time Malory and I followed them out, both Davies and his pursuer were nowhere in sight.

We raced down to the hotel lobby. All we found was the young cop, whose name, I recollected, was Calder. He was out of breath and there was no sign of Lew Davies. Malory, naturally angry at himself, proceeded to take it out on Calder.

"You let him get away! We had him right there in the room, now he could be anywhere!"

Calder controlled himself admirably, pleading, "He just disappeared. But we'll have the place searched in minutes. We'll get him."

"Minutes is all he needs," I said sceptically. This case had too many chases up and down halls and back stairwells for my liking. I wasn't up for any more of this kind of nonsense. My interest in pursuing Davies was nil. That was the cops' job. I'd done mine.

"Well, I brought him in. It's up to you to hold him. Good night," I said. Malory looked startled. It hadn't occurred to him that not everyone is interested in a manhunt.

"Hey, wait a minute," he began, then considered for a second. "Oh, OK. Plenty of time tomorrow. Good night." His busy mind was on the fugitive, on the excitement of the chase.

I went back to Sonia's suite. The place was in an uproar. Sterling was still on the phone. He looked at me, I shook my head. He continued talking, his hand covering his mouth so we couldn't hear the mysterious police jargon. Sonia was crying on Betty's shoulder. Alex and Walter talked quietly in one corner. I joined them. In spite of myself I was also angry so I interrupted.

"Well, you've maneouvred yourself from prime murder suspect to material witness, in one easy, silly bit of exhibitionism. Pleased with yourself?"

Lauker laughed in my face and proceeded to gloat.

"It's an improvement, right. See here. If I'd told that story to the cops while under arrest, I'd still be under arrest. Nobody would've believed it. They'd see it as just an attempt to get myself off the hook."

"Well, wasn't it?"

"No, now they have to take me and my story seriously. Davies gave himself away, that's a bonus. He's a fugitive. I don't mind being a witness. It'll be fun." He gave me full benefit of his large, uneven teeth. His blue eyes were bright with excitement.

During this exchange Sterling finished his calls; Betty and Sonia had turned and were listening in. Alex took the situation in at a glance.

"Stop it you two. That's enough. Everyone go home. Sonia needs her rest."

Superintendent Sterling hurried to agree.

"Miss Keremos, there is nothing more you can do here now. Leave this to us. I'll have one of my men drive Mr. Lauker and Miss Grelick home. You need rest too. This has been a strain. Plenty of time tomorrow." He rambled on, his manner suddenly fatherly, but I listened to only half of what he said.

"Yes, take this bum out of here. Betty will stay, we'll look after getting her home."

Sterling got the message. He motioned to Walter Lauker. Surprisingly, Lauker allowed himself to be led away with just a short goodnight to Sonia. We were left alone, Sonia, Betty, Alex and I.

It could've developed into a four-way klatsch but Alex wouldn't allow her patient to stay up. She persuaded a fading Sonia to take a sleeping pill and go to bed. All I did was watch them disappear into Sonia's bedroom.

Once Betty and I were alone in the livingroom she took my hand, her face white and drawn.

"This is terrible. I don't believe it's happening—" She would have gone on but like a fool I interrupted impatiently, "It's happening, it's happening. Believe it. Now we've got Lew to worry about. I need a drink. Look, I'm so tired I can't think. However, on the chance that the cops don't get him tonight, where would he go? You know him, where would he go, whom would he go to for help, hiding? Think!"

"That's easy. He would come to either me or Sonia. We are his friends, best he has. So—"

"Sonia's hardly in a position to hide him. And you'll be watched, you know. If the cops don't get him tonight there will be a stakeout at your place and anywhere Lew Davies is known to have a friend. Right?"

"Yes, yes. So what do we do?"

"Think about it. I can't keep my eyes open any more and my brain is mush. Could be that he'll contact his coke connection—" Betty didn't answer, and I looked at the phone doubtfully. What a bind not to be able to call Nate Ottoline and discuss this with him over the phone! But that was out of the question. The risks to Nate were too great. I heaved myself up from the couch, put down my drink and called him anyway. Just to tell him I could use his help. I was lucky, I guess. He was 'available' right away. He and Ronnie promised to join Alex and me, while Sonia slept. I suggested to Betty that she go home and sit tight.

"And expect to be watched. If Lew is smart he'll lie low tonight, in a ravine or garage. By tomorrow—we'll see. Go get some sleep. Tomorrow we must deal with the $200,000 extortion demand as well as everything else. It will be a big day."

My mind was racing again, temporarily stimulated by that drink on an empty stomach. Betty looked at me.

"You should be in bed. You know that, don't you. You're exhausted and look it."

"Yeah, I know. But we must be ready. Sooner the better. Please. Believe me and do what I ask."

"OK. But under protest," Betty said.

"Noted, noted. Now go!"

Reluctantly she left. I was relieved to see her go.

Alex, Ronnie, Nate and I sat up talking for long weary hours after Sonia was asleep and Betty had gone home. Perhaps because of my tiredness it took longer than necessary to get our act together. We talked about Davies and Lauker but the extortion demand kept intruding. From the timing it could have been Karl Deerfield just before he was killed. But it was doubtful. Why would he change tactics? And it didn't jibe with the story Karl allegedly told Walter. Apart from Karl, it was open season; it could've been anybody. Karl's original accomplice or someone piggybacking—grasping the opportunity to cash in on the bombing. Nothing to do but have the money on hand and wait for the follow-up call. Time and place. Could be interesting. It was agreed that Ronnie would stick around next day in case he was needed.

Then we mulled over the case against Davies and the significance of his flight. Panic? He would've been better off to sit tight and deny everything. It was Sonia's acceptance of Walter's story that had spooked him. Which didn't amount to an admission of guilt. Not necessarily.

We had come to the conclusion that if Lew eluded the police he would definitely make another attempt to see Sonia. To explain, and get back into her good graces. Hence our preparations to make it easy for him to do that. Hence—well, this idea would certainly occur to Malory. The hotel would be swarming with cops. So, something would have to be done about that. That was to be my job. Nate was to check up on Davies' coke connection, just in case that proved to be a lead.

It wasn't until early in the morning that we finally got to discuss Sedgwick, Bono and Weller.

"Everyone seems to have forgotten those three. Where do they fit in this mess?" said Alex at one point.

"They aren't all one bunch any more. And it's hard to fit any of them in with either Davies or Lauker. It's a different connection somehow. But you're right, we have to get to them sometime soon. Is Davies likely to contact any of them? Bono maybe?"

"I'll get Sonia to ask them all around to see her tomorrow. Perhaps we can start something."

That was my contribution. Not great but all I could think of at the time. Of course Alex wouldn't let me get away with it.

"Is that the best you can do? That's not the old Helen Keremos we know and love."

"Correct. I'm bushed. Besides, I've never had a case like this. I feel that I'm constantly missing something."

"I'll tell you one thing that's different about this case. You've taken to believing your client. In fact you've fallen for your client. That's not like you, is it?"

"You have a point, definitely a point. I'll take it under advisement. Anything else? No. Then let's wrap it up." I couldn't handle any more.

26

NEXT DAY I HAD TO make myself human again. After a large breakfast and a long hot tub I went out onto Yonge Street, leaving Alex to look after the still sleeping Sonia. I had myself a long overdue haircut which trimmed my thick, black hair to manageable length. Then I bought a gorgeous shirt and indulged myself further by having a friendly masseuse work on my long-suffering back and arms for a good hour. For the first time in days I felt smart, strong and spiffy. A good feeling. Perhaps an illusion, but much needed.

After my shopping trip I made my way to see Malory. Lew Davies was still 'at large'; Sonia's new lawyers—not Sedgwick's crowd, you can bet—were in there pitching for both Davies and Lauker; Sonia and Alex were safe in the hotel; there was no word from Betty. And Malory was plenty mad.

Which was understandable. It's hard shit to have an explosive case, which you believed safely closed, suddenly reopen with a bang and then have the new suspect vanish right before your eyes. It's bad for morale and even worse for the career. So I was almost sympathetic to the poor guy. Enough to make Malory comfortable about confiding his troubles to me.

"See here. We don't really have anything on this Davies. He said a stupid thing, but so what? It would never stand up as a confession. Sure he split and is hiding out. Presumption of guilt, and all that. Naturally we must find him and get some questions answered. We're checking for any connection between him and Karl Deerfield and I bet we'll come up with something. But charge him with murder— on Lauker's say so? No way. Would you? Anyway it's not up to me. Upstairs, they're still conferring. They may go for Lauker; they may go for Davies. Either way we've got to get him. No question about that."

"Then pull your men away from the hotel. Davies would have to be blind to come within miles of it. The lobby is full of idle men in polyester pants and lumpy jackets."

"Isn't it always?"

"Not such lumpy jackets," I answered.

"Funny, aren't we? You know I can't leave the hotel uncovered. But I'll have them play it coy, if you think that will help." Which only proved that he was stumped and angry. I left him, satisfied.

By the time I was through with Malory, Alex and Sonia were playing backgammon in Sonia's bedroom. Ronnie was in the livingroom carefully observing the constant stream of messengers and room service employees—food, champagne, flowers, get-well cards—and curious visitors, mostly from the music scene. I was glad someone was keeping track of it all. I noted the comings and goings, the hustle, the phone calls. Something, someone was missing. It took me a moment to realize that I was missing the take-charge skills of Lew Davies. But that wasn't what felt so wrong. It was the absence of Betty which was disturbing me.

Why wasn't she here? It was past noon and she hadn't shown up. Then it struck me. How stupid could I get! A haircut and a new shirt hadn't helped enough. I was missing all the obvious things. I recalled the night before and Betty's comment, "He would come to either me or Sonia. We're his best friends." Of course! I walked quickly into my room and almost pounced on the private phone. I called Betty. No answer. I called Nate. No answer. I called Malory. A calm, official voice informed me that Sergeant Malory was unavailable, would I like to leave a message? No. I had nothing to say. Only questions. Was there a guard on Betty? Probably. Had they reported? Why was Malory unavailable, I fumed. I was just hyping myself up to look for Betty myself when Sonia called me from the next room.

"Did I tell you? Ben and Chuck came to see me this morning. Bet they waited in the lobby until you went out. Anyway, they wanted this and that. Ben still comes on to me like I was a vestal virgin or something. I should marry him as soon as possible so he can take me away from all this. That's his line.

No mention of Arthur. But it was real clear, both Ben and Chuck want Arthur's scalp. Funny how quickly they turned against him. He was their idol and now—they would destroy him if they could. Anyway, I said that I'll get one of these sharp women lawyers to look into a civil suit against Sedgwick. And then I told them to get lost. How am I doing?"

"Good, real good. Will Weller cooperate in a suit against Sedgwick?"

"If I pay him enough. He needs money but also he's scared of Sedgwick. I told him I wouldn't give him a cent. He said he couldn't take the risk otherwise. So finally they both left."

"Without specifics of Sedgwick's deal with Universal Sound you'll never make your suit stick. I might be able to come up with something. It would sure be nice to make mincemeat of Arthur T. Sedgwick, Q.C.," I replied.

"Oh, I don't care whether I win against him or not. But I would like to throw a scare into him. And then to be out of it all. Since the Universal contract is a put-up job it looks like my so-called career is bust anyway. All I want is never to see any of them again."

"Even Ben Bono? He wasn't in on Sedgwick's contract scam."

"Especially Ben Bono. He doesn't know me or want to. I hadn't realized that until today. I hadn't realized a lot of things." Sonia looked at me. Before I could react, she added, "Where's Betty? Why isn't she here?"

"I don't know. But on a hunch she's gone to meet Davies somewhere."

"God, yes! Obviously he would turn to her. Why hadn't I been up front with you about Betty and Lew! I knew they were cooking something together, some dope deal, probably. I'm not sure just what it amounted to but they were in it together. So now that Lew is in hiding, Betty would help him. For sure. Just as I would, if I could." Sonia's voice dropped guiltily.

"Anything else you haven't told me? Now's the time to come clean." I was dead serious. Not angry but seriously concerned by Alex's accusation that my feelings for Sonia were clouding my judgment. "How about that money you've been paying Lauker every month. It keeps bugging me."

She considered the question.

"Alimony would be a figure of speech. I just wanted to give him something, no strings attached. He never asked for it."

"But $500! You sure he wouldn't find it downright insulting? I think I would."

"Would you? But you aren't Walt. I don't know how he felt about it, he never said. D'you think I'm cheap not to make it more?"

"It doesn't matter what I think you are. But Lauker matters. How about that story he told on Davies. You believe Davies killed Karl?"

Sonia didn't answer. Her world was disintegrating around her. Sedgwick and the Universal fiasco; Bono and Weller, Grelick and Davies, all of whom had their own agendas. And Lauker. Since she couldn't trust them, naturally she turned to me for help and support. Perhaps more. But I had to concentrate on the case, had to keep my personal feelings out of it. I had to keep up the pressure. End the case first, despite not only my feelings, but hers.

"Sonia, this is no time to fall apart. You seemed to believe Lauker. That's what caused Davies to act like a fool and take off like he did. Why? Why believe Lauker rather than Davies? Isn't it six of one and half a dozen of the other?"

"I don't know why. Maybe because I never expected anything serious from Walt. He just bops along. And murder is serious. Lew is different. He's a fine, dedicated musician. He cares, he accomplishes things. I can't really think of either of them as murderers but it's especially hard with Walt. He's such a baby really. And he was my husband."

"The baby who was your husband. Hm." I thought of Walter Lauker. His apartment, his flamboyance, his bullshit, his cute little socks. He didn't strike me as an innocent. But then I hadn't been married to him. I shuddered at the very thought.

"Helen, go find Betty. If Lew is the murderer, she isn't safe.

She mustn't get involved any more than she is already. And not in helping him escape, dear god. It's mad!"

My fears about Sonia appeared to be needless, she wasn't about to fall apart. On the contrary she was thinking clearly and giving orders. I nodded and agreed gladly.

"OK. But first we have to decide what to do about that $200,000. Did you get it? Where is it?"

Sonia lay on a nest of pillows, a bright green afghan around her shoulders. She grinned, lifted herself up and moved the pillows. Behind her was a smart new packsack. It looked full. Two hundred thousand dollars in small bills take up a lot of space.

"The trust company assistant manager and a security guard brought it while you were out. She tried to get me to tell her what I wanted it for. I told her it wasn't any business of theirs. She made me sign about six different receipts and disclaimers so the trust company wouldn't take any flack no matter what happens. So there it is."

"You've been busy this morning. Good. So we're all ready."

As I spoke Alex walked in. She looked concerned:

"Sorry to interrupt. Malory is here. He wants to talk to Helen. Right away. He doesn't look happy. In fact he's being obnoxious."

Malory was in the livingroom being studiously ignored by Ronnie. I invited him into my bedroom and closed the door. He was at his most cop-like. Impressive. Intimidating. Pompous. He started in on me.

"Miss Keremos, I've been very cooperative with you. Indulgent in fact. I must warn you that your actions in this case are unacceptable." He stopped and glared at me.

"What's biting you, Sergeant? You got a rocket from upstairs for allowing Davies to skedaddle and you want somebody to blame! Why take it out on me?" This didn't go over very big.

"Yesterday you evaded surveillance. This directly affected our ability to place Davies in custody."

"Oh, balls! What's that got to do with anything? Davies wasn't under surveillance. I was. Why was I? Why wasn't

— *149* —

Davies? You boobed. Admit it and let's get on with it."

"Further, it has been reported that a considerable sum of money has been withdrawn from Miss Deerfield's account. Would you care to explain that?"

"I would care to explain nothing. You want to know about Sonia's money, ask her. Not that it's any of your business. I hope she spits in your eye."

"I suggest that you warn her. If any of that money ends up in the hands of the fugitive Lew Davies, Miss Deerfield could be charged with being an accessory."

This was getting too much.

"Oh, come off it, Malory! Quit this act. Where's your Actors' Equity card?" I said. "Does it make sense to alienate both Sonia and me because your feelings are hurt and Davies got away from you? Now, does it?"

Unpersuaded, Malory burst out, "Nuts. It's not only Davies. I'm tired of spoiled, glamourous millionaires; high-priced, snooty lawyers; smart-ass female snoops..."

"OK, OK. What's happened? Tell me. Spit it out in Mama's hand, you'll feel better."

"Elizabeth Grelick's disappeared. Oh, we had a tail on her, never fear. For protection, like. We lost her, damn it. Or rather Davies faked us out. Now, if you or Miss Deerfield or those buddies of yours Alex Edwards or Nate Ottoline had any hand in this—there'll be hell to pay."

"No chance. We all missed the obvious. Did he snatch her?"

"Snatch her? I don't know. It's possible. He made contact by phone. Gobbledy gook. We couldn't make it out. Next thing we know she's out of her apartment and in the Eaton Centre. Now you try to find anyone at the Eaton Centre! It's impossible. She obviously knew just where to meet him. We combed the whole place as best we could. No dice. You have to know more about this scene than I do, so I came here."

"And proceeded to let off steam at me. I get it. OK. Truce. You'll need me. Well?"

"Yes. We've got to get Davies. With or without Grelick. I don't care. She could be just a sentimental broad. They're always being used by some prick or other and taking a fall. She isn't important, it's Davies I want. Is he going to come here to see Sonia, or what? What's your guess?"

"He'll be here. Because he's an arrogant prick who's always conning some sentimental broad or other." I couldn't resist the dig. "He thinks he can go on conning Sonia if he's given a chance. His ego feeds on it. Like Lauker's. Like yours—"

"OK. Sorry I started it. You said 'truce'. Look, let's drop it. Let's cooperate. I've pulled my men. They're well under cover. No more lumpy jackets in the hotel lobby. Now, who the hell is that guy in the livingroom? Private bodyguard? He doesn't look like he could swat a fly." Malory meant Ronnie, who sat peacefully watching Sonia's bedroom door and doing his manicure. I laughed.

"He's better than a SWAT team. He doesn't look like a cop, no way. That's why he won't spook Davies. Leave it to us. In spite of your cracks we have to proceed on the assumption that Betty Grelick is an innocent hostage. Even if not innocent, we don't want her or anyone to get hurt. So we have to be careful with Davies. Who knows what his state of mind is right now? He could do something rash. Agreed?"

"Agreed. I don't know about rash. The guy is smart. Very. He has brains, chutzpa and connections. If she is a hostage, where is he stashing her? Tell me that. Unless he has friends. Friends who would go out on a limb for him. Know of any?"

"Yes. In there, in the bedroom, lying in bed. That's another reason he'll come here. That's settled then. Now what about Sedgwick. Do I get him?"

"God, don't you ever give up?" He pretended ennui. "OK, come to my office about ten forty-five tomorrow. I'll be going over Weller's testimony. I'm a busy man, liable to be called away at any time."

I nodded, satisfied. He would leave me alone with Weller's file for long enough to get names, dates and other details. After that it would be up to me and Sonia's lawyers.

"It's a deal," I said. "And for that I'll give you something. It may not be much but who knows. Have you looked carefully at that hotel receipt I got from Karl Deerfield's room?"

"No, not what I would call carefully. By the time you saw fit to give it to me Karl was dead and we knew he'd been at the hotel. There wasn't any point—" His uncertainty was touching.

"You're supposed to be a detective, my friend. The Imperial Palace Hotel charges $68 for two in a room. A single is only $64."

"So he wasn't alone. Who do you suppose was there with him? That was the time Miss Deerfield's apartment was vandalized." Malory was quick to see the possibilities.

"He would need a lookout, it seems to me. Not so?"

"Possibly, possibly. But who?"

"Get Chester on it. If he can't get a line on who it was, your boys sure as hell won't."

Malory ignored the crack. Just nodded and said, "If we could pin it down to Davies. That would be something to be getting on with!"

"Something. So now you owe me one."

"Well, in case you're still interested in the explosion that almost wiped you and Sonia out—" It was his turn to grin at me.

"I'd almost forgotten. So what's new on that?"

"Well, the bomb boys are sure the charge was plenty big enough to kill you. You and anyone else in the vehicle. They aren't sure how it was set off and they don't know how you survived. But it would've blown you apart had you been moving and with a seatbelt on."

"That's cheerful news. I'll think on that. Sonia would've died too. Hmm." Something was stirring in the back of my mind. I wanted to sit down alone and let it percolate but that's not the way my business works. As soon as Malory left (without seeing Sonia about the money) Alex was on to me.

"A call just came in. It was Betty. With a message. You're to take the $200,000 and go to the last place you and she met. That's the Ritz, right? The cops won't know that. Go at once. Don't bring a tail. You'll be contacted."

"Is she OK? Is she in it with Davies or did she have a gun to her head?" I asked. Alex shrugged.

"I'm not psychic," she said. "What bothers me is how you're going to get out of the hotel with that great pack on your back without alerting every cop in sight. They may not be obvious but they are around. Count on it."

"Sure. But that's not much of a problem." I turned to Ronnie. He's a slight, soft-spoken young man with gently curling hair, a gold ring in one ear and a deceptively mild manner. "Malory didn't know about you when he got here. Chances are good he didn't think to give you a tail. Take that pack and meet me at the corner of Yonge and Charles."

Ronnie was pleased. He wanted to be useful.

"Maybe right in the Charles Street Promenade would be less noticeable," he suggested, struggling into the pack.

"OK. Wander around like a tourist. The place is stiff with them. I'll approach you when I know it's safe. Good luck," I said.

"Break a leg," said Alex. Ronnie smiled at us and left.

27

I HAD THE TAXI let me off at the corner of Charles Street at Bay rather than Yonge Street where Davies might be expecting me, and walked east. I didn't believe he'd be at the Ritz. Too easy to get bottled up in that tiny place. So he would hang about outside planning to come up behind me. I walked slowly towards Yonge Street past the hole-in-the-wall entrance to the Ritz. No sign of Davies. At the Yonge corner, I looked around, spotted Ronnie just entering the Promenade, looking beautifully part of the scenery. Yonge Street was crowded as it always is. I started to cross Charles going north, together with half a hundred other pedestrians. Davies was good. The first I knew of his presence was a poke in the ribs. And there he was, smiling through his teeth, his hand with something hard in it under my arm.

"Keep walking. I'll steer. That's a gun," he said in my ear.

"I didn't think it was a bunch of roses. What's it for?" I asked.

"Don't ask stupid questions. Where's the money?"

"Near, very near. If you let me go I'll lead you to it. Or get it for you, as you like."

"Why don't you have it with you?" he demanded. By now we were standing in front of the Promenade entrance. Davies was restless; moving from foot to foot, looking around, his gun hand trembling slightly in my armpit. Not a good scene. I contemplated trying to get the gun away from him; decided the risk was too great. The crowds were thick around us; besides I didn't fancy having a hole blown in my side. So there we were, standing on the sidewalk like dummies. Davies was stymied. He'd had a plan all worked out and couldn't cope with the unexpected fact that I didn't have the money on me. I had to take the initiative or we would never get anywhere.

Gently, slowly I disengaged my arm, careful not to alarm him and give him any reason to pull the trigger.

"Look, Lew, this is bloody ridiculous. It was hard enough to sneak out of the hotel without a bevy of cops on my tail. To carry a bag of money as well was impossible. A friend, someone whom the police don't know, has got it. He's inside the Promenade." I had Davies' full attention. "So let me go in there. I'll get the dough and walk slowly any direction you say. You can pick me up again whenever you like. How about it?"

He really didn't have a hell of a lot of choice if his priority was the money. I wondered what he was on. Whatever it was, it wasn't helping his concentration. He took a few seconds to think about the money. It turned out not to be of first importance to him.

"No. Forget the money. Let's walk." He grabbed my arm again and propelled me back down the street.

What would Ronnie do now? Go back to the hotel? Or try and follow us? I wasn't sure I wanted that. But there wasn't much I could do about it without having Davies shoot up the street.

It was a fine afternoon on Yonge Street. We walked cosily arm in arm among the late lunchtime crowd. It would've been easy to meet someone who knew one of us. I wondered about that. Davies steered me around the corner then up again on the next block. We were moving towards Bloor Street. The bulk of the Manulife Centre with its posh stores, fountains, escalators and a multitude of exits and entrances loomed before us. I thought of the Eaton Centre about ten blocks south, where Betty had disappeared. Toronto is honeycombed with large shopping and office complexes, underground malls, and under-street passages. Davies was using them to good effect. Smart boy.

We came abreast of an entrance to the Manulife Centre. Davies looked around—so did I, Ronnie wasn't in sight—and we ducked into it. Still in silence, we made our circuitous way to a door marked STAIRS. It led down to the underground parking garage and public washrooms. Davies still hugged me affectionately. Nobody saw us, nobody noticed anything wrong. Why should they?

One flight down the door to the GENTLEMEN had an OUT OF SERVICE sign on it. That was it!

Betty was there locked in one of the cubicles, with a mass of tissue in her mouth, kept in place by a red bandana, her hands tied behind her. Davies pushed me into the next cubicle, and told me to sit down. Then he backed off. With the doors open he could watch us both. Sitting in a tight space, my movement and view were badly restricted.

"Don't try anything, Helen. I'm going to untie Betty. It must be uncomfortable for her. Then we can talk."

"No sweat. I'm not going anywhere."

Minutes later Betty was spitting tissue into the basin and washing her face. Davies watched me.

"I want to see Sonia. And I want out of the murder rap. Betty has promised to help. Will you?"

"Why should I?"

"I've Betty as hostage. Remember that. You must get me in to see Sonia so I can explain. I'm in a spot. I've little enough to lose. Well?"

"Nuts. Lew, don't be a fool. You split when Lauker accused you of murdering Deerfield. That was dumb. It's his word against yours what happened in that apartment. Give yourself up, then you can explain all you want."

"No. I don't trust the cops. Or Lauker. He's turned Sonia against me. I must see her privately. Soon."

"Lauker's accusation isn't all there is, is it? There are the calls, extortion and the bomb. That's what you're afraid of."

Lew Davies moved his gun hand impatiently.

"I don't intend to discuss it with you."

Betty Grelick had been standing still by the basin listening to our exchange. Then she broke in.

"You must, Lew, you must. We have to tell Helen! Tell her everything. It's our only chance. Don't you see that?" Without waiting for his reply she continued: "Helen, you must help us. Not just Lew but both of us. You see we started these calls to Sonia—"

Davies shouted, "You stupid bitch! I tried to keep you out

of it, we agreed on this plan. What's the matter with you! We can't trust this bird, she's working with the cops!" He was reverting, his vocabulary deteriorating. Grelick was calm. On the surface, at least.

"Lew, it won't work. Just tell Helen what we were going to tell Sonia. Then she'll help us. I know she will."

"Do you? I don't." He was shouting again. I sat perfectly still letting them work it out between them.

"I don't think we've got any choice any longer." By contrast, Betty spoke softly. "You can't expect Helen to believe that I'm an innocent hostage. So you can't use me that way."

"Oh, can't I! Just watch me. Go on, get in there and sit down." Davies waved his gun at Betty, motioning her into the adjacent cubicle. She didn't move.

"No, Lew," she said. The tableau froze for a moment. Lew Davies' plan had turned to ratshit. What would he do now? He wasn't good at dealing with the unexpected.

"Betty's right, you know, Lew. Relax and tell me the whole story. I promise to listen and get Sonia to listen to you."

There was a tense moment while Lew Davies considered.

"All right, all right then. I can't fight both of you. Besides, it'll be a relief."

So that's how I came to hear the story of Betty Grelick's and Lew Davies' involvement in the Deerfield case against a background of urinals in a can at Toronto's Manulife Centre. If the location was less than inspiring, the story was worse. The mess that people can get themselves into!

"You heard how Sedgwick, Bono and Weller muscled in on us. Betty and I had very mixed feelings about it all along. Part of it was OK, Sonia was getting better gigs, it seemed like her career could be taking off. And that's what we all wanted. Listen, whatever you think, whatever we did, whatever I did, it was all for Sonia," Lew Davies pleaded.

"Yes, yes. Granted. Go on," I assured him.

"As long as you understand that. Well, then, it became more and more clear that Sedgwick was running things. He was in total charge. Sonia let him. No question that a lawyer with his connections is useful to a career. But it was like nothing could happen without him; like he was creating Sonia. We're just flunkies. We went along; it was no use talking to Sonia, she was mesmerized. He's a powerful man, you know. Personally as well as professionally. We hoped it would all work out, that we could use him and his connections without getting totally swallowed up. But it got worse and worse. Then Sonia won that lottery. A million dollars! Think of it! Well, we figured, now we don't need Sedgwick, now we can go back to just the three of us. What happened then was amazing. I still don't understand it. After an initial flurry everything went back to square one. Sonia only showed her independence by putting the money in a private account. Then nothing. It was as if the win never happened. Sedgwick dangled that Universal contract. Weller and Bono busily made plans, arrangements, bossing us all around. So Betty and I decided we had to keep reminding Sonia about that million. We came up with the idea of making calls."

I interrupted.

"What did you think it would accomplish? After all, she might have just turned it over to Sedgwick to administer."

"Oh, we made sure she realized that wouldn't get her off the hook. Anyway, we didn't think she would do that, she was sort of proud of not having turned it over to them in the first place. Anyway—" Betty broke in.

"Anyway, we never thought about it until after we'd started. Let's be up front about it. We just went ahead as a joke almost. Then the possibilities began to hit us. Like, that we could get our hands on some of that money. Come on, Lew, quit kidding yourself. The idea had occurred."

"Yes, I admit it started to occur to us we could do things with some of that million. I had a deal cooking which needed some cash, and Betty kept coming up with publicity ideas for Sonia. But we never went anywhere with it. For one thing we didn't know how to get Sonia to cooperate. She was in Sedgwick's pocket and never did anything without his say so. That million got to be taboo. She couldn't deal with being a millionaire. The few calls we made didn't seem to do anything except worry her and make her less sure of herself. So we were just about ready to back off when Karl Deerfield approached us."

"How he'd found out what we were doing I never knew, but he did. He had a scam and he made us a proposition. We were to concentrate on persuading Sonia to let him be her personal financial advisor like Weller and that lot were her professional advisors. He made it sound very proper and natural on the basis of being her uncle, her only male relative."

"And you fell for it! My god, you're nuts! Didn't you pick up that Sonia wasn't exactly crazy about him?"

"Well, we didn't exactly fall for it, we just had very little choice. He threatened to expose us, tell Sonia a whole cock-and-bull story about what greedy disloyal schemers we were."

"Really." I looked at the pair of them. Betty was huddled in one corner, close to tears. The spunk she had shown had evaporated, overwhelmed by the implications of this sorry story. Lew wasn't much better. Both realized what a morass they had gotten themselves into. Starting as an altruistic joke, the lure of big money had inexorably led them to this. Events and other people's schemes had taken the game out of their hands and produced murder.

"Go on," I said.

"Karl Deerfield took over. He made the phone calls, I gave him information. It was his idea to make use of the coincidental purse snatching and auto accident. But he said it wasn't enough. Something had to happen right in Sonia's apartment. So we planned the vandalism." Lew's eyes pleaded for mercy. He looked over at Betty who shook her head.

"I didn't. You guys cooked that one all by yourselves. I wouldn't."

"Yes, OK, Betty wasn't in that. Anyway it backfired. Sonia freaked out and you got hired. And that's all! That's all we ever did! I didn't know anything about the bomb. But it looks bad. If the cops trace our connection with Karl we're done for."

"Maybe. Anyway, not 'we', just you, Lew," I said. "What

happened at Walter's apartment the night Karl Deerfield was murdered? That's the operative question."

"Nothing much while I was there. You were so insistent on finding Karl I thought I'd better get to him first. I knew he meant to go see Walt. He was losing his grip and I was afraid of what he might do or say. I was damn scared. When I got to Walt's place I found them talking and getting smashed together. So I had one drink and left. I never hit Walter or Karl. I swear! But how can I prove it?"

"You don't have to prove you didn't do it, but it sure didn't help to lose your nerve and split when Walt accused you in front of Sonia and the cops. For a bright lad you acted real stupid. Making it all the worse for yourself. And now you've brought Betty into it. Nice going. This phony hostage bit. It's childish."

"Yes, I guess it is. But we couldn't think of anything else to do. I want a chance to explain to Sonia. Sans cops. If she won't or can't help me then Betty and I will take the money and try to get out of the country."

"You've been watching too many TV dramas. By the way, did you make that original extortion call yesterday afternoon?"

"No. That was Karl. Must have been. We just took advantage of his call to try to get our hands on that money. I guess we were naive. Now look at this mess!"

"Yeah, it isn't tidy, that's for sure. What next?"

Lew Davies walked up to my cozy little cubicle and got extra earnest.

"Get us in to see Sonia. Somehow. I know you can do it. Between us we can con the cops. Please. Give us half an hour with her. Then we'll decide what to do next."

"And the money? Don't you need it to feed your habit?"

"Later, we'll decide all that later," Betty broke in impatiently. "Never mind anything else. Now, will you help us?"

"Yes," I said. "I'll take you to see Sonia. Without the police. Then let her decide what next. Got a car? And I don't mean that white Volvo or Betty's BMW."

"Sure we have a car. An old orange Datsun. In the parking

garage right under us here. But how d'you plan to get us in to see Sonia with the cops all over that hotel?"

"Here's the scoop. Listen carefully. It's simple and clean." I told them my plan. Simple and clean it was. They looked at each other. Then Davies nodded.

"Good. That should work. Don't doublecross us."

I didn't bother to answer. We left together. I went up to the mall, they down to the garage.

28

FIFTEEN MINUTES LATER I was back in the hotel on Jarvis Street, dealing with a worried Alex and an angry Malory. Ronnie feigned sleep on the livingroom couch, the money sack was nowhere to be seen.

Malory frothed at the mouth a bit and swore to arrest everyone in sight, especially me. It took a good hour to get him calmed down and on his way with assurances that Lew Davies badly wanted to see Sonia and would therefore show up. As I expected he was skeptical about Betty being a 'real' hostage. But he went along.

My talk with Sonia was brief. I told her to get lots of rest and not to worry. Everything was under control. Gratefully she pretended to believe me. Alex gave her another sleeping pill and by eight she was asleep. So far so good.

I sat in my room for a while after that, thinking. Ronnie had gone home, the pack sack was in my care. The plan I had suggested to Betty and Lew wasn't to go into operation until the early hours of next morning. The smart thing would have been to take a shower and go to bed. I took a shower. Alex came in to watch me dress.

"So you're off again. What is it this time?"

I sat on the bed putting on my shoes. I could feel the tension in my arms and legs which the quick shower couldn't dissipate. My body knew the case was coming to a climax and knew also that much would be demanded of it before the end.

"Alex, give me an answer off the top of your head. Is Sonia divorced or not?"

"Not, I think. Just separated."

"Right. Then who inherits in the event of her death?"

"Walter Lauker!"

"Right. That's why I'm going out."

"Wow," said Alex.

I don't know why it had taken me this long to clue in on Lauker's misdirection. His use of Karl Deerfield to put us off the track had been masterly. His arrest was a stroke of genius. It concentrated everything on a conspiracy between him and Karl—a conspiracy which was absurd, had never existed and therefore didn't stand up. As it disintegrated so did the murder charge against Lauker. It's not always enough to have the right murderer; you've got to have the right case, right motive, right circumstances. We had missed the obvious by a country mile. Precisely because it was so obvious. The spouse inherits. It was as simple as that, I was sure of it. All else was sleight of hand. All of Walter Lauker's disarming cuteness was camouflage. So he wouldn't be taken seriously. Sonia said it all—"Murder is serious, Walt isn't." People who don't care whether their socks match aren't likely to be suspected of perpetrating complex plots. We had been conned by our own stereotypes.

"And let that be a lesson to us all," I grinned up at Alex as we concluded our examination of Lauker's role in the case. I got up, stretched, said goodbye to her and left the suite. On my way out I dropped in on Chester. Ever since the explosion and especially since the murder of Karl Deerfield, Chester and his precious hotel had been the target for snoopy reporters and assorted thrill seekers. As Chester was our first line of defence against them it behooved me to give him an occasional pat on the back as one colleague to another. That took me ten minutes. Finally I was free for my third invasion of Walter Lauker's theatre of the absurd, his Annex flat.

Walter, accompanied by his cat Herod, was busy removing all semblance of order which the compulsive police had inadvertently introduced into his bizarre stage. At my entrance he immediately began to make coffee and regale me with his triumphs over the criminal justice system.

"Did you hear? They dropped the charges. I got a handsome apology from Sterling to boot." He was bursting with pleasure, as well he might. On a real high. It was going to be my pleasure to bring him down.

"Humph," I replied.

He ignored my lack of enthusiasm.

"I really should thank you. You helped, you really did. Can I offer you anything out of my humble collection of instant antiques as a thank you gift? Perhaps this?" He picked up a pale green object which at a pinch could have served as a flower vase. "It's so very feminine, so very 'you', don't you agree? Or even better, this." Up came a dingy portrait of Queen Victoria in a tacky modern frame. "Completely useless. But nice, don't you think?"

"Walter, it's over," I said, in turn ignoring his performance.

"Oh? What's over, my dear Helen?"

"The charade. Your charade. You didn't think it could go on forever, did you? You're through."

He wasn't fazed a bit, as far as I could see.

"So you think I'm through, do you. How very silly of you. What gives you that idea?"

"You did kill Karl Deerfield. Just after Lew Davies left. First you pumped Karl, then Davies arrived. A godsend. You saw the possibilities immediately. Get rid of a dangerous Karl who was distraught and raving, make an obvious fall guy of yourself and then point at Davies as Karl's co-conspirator. Perfect. It took guts, I grant you. To get arrested and hold out on the cops until you could stage that production in front of Sonia and Lew. With everyone present, including even a police superintendent. You couldn't be sure Lew would be such a damn fool. His running was a bonus."

"Not at all. I've been studying Lew for years. I knew he would break. He was bound to feel guilty and then run. And now it's done. The cops have tied him to Karl. With your help. He's a cinch for the murder." He was still up there in the clouds, fascinated by his own cleverness, but there was more tension around his mouth. A vein pulsed in his forehead.

"Walt. You're good at illusions, magic tricks, conjuring. But you know better than I that once a trick has been explained and the house lights go on, the illusion is over. Your scenery is painted, the magic gone. It's over, Walter, finished for ever."

He appeared to consider.

"Never really thought I could fool you for long. That's why I thought it was such a good idea when Karl suggested blowing up your truck. It would have been so nice and simple had both you and Sonia bought it then. Too bad it didn't work." His regret was palpable. "Even as it stands, you knowing and you proving are two very, very different things. You see, I never actually DID anything. Except kill old Deerfield, of course. But that will be hard to prove, with Lew the perfect suspect, right on the premises at the time. He's a much better candidate than I am. After all, he and Karl were after Sonia's money. They actually met, they plotted together, they made calls. I didn't. So there is good evidence against Lew. Nothing against me."

"Got to admire your ability to kid yourself. Tell me, how did you intend to kill Sonia? That was the ultimate goal wasn't it? The bomb didn't do it. It would have been perfect to become a bereaved husband without taking any risks. You can't hope to have such an opportunity again."

"I've been thinking about that. And I've come up with a perfectly good plan. Risky, that I'll admit, but creative. Very creative. Well, this conversation has been most stimulating but Herod and I need our beauty sleep. Reluctantly, we must bid you adieu. Very good night to you."

Walter was graciousness itself. His hurry to get rid of me was understandable. But his use of the present and future tenses, when speaking about killing Sonia, chilled me to the bone.

"Pleasant dreams," I said, pretending I hadn't noticed anything.

29

I WAKENED SONIA at five a.m. She had been asleep for nine hours and declared herself to be sufficiently recuperated to deal with what was required of her. We went over my plan in detail. Sonia rose to the occasion as I knew she would, dressed quietly and was ready in minutes.

At this time of the morning the hotel kitchen opens, the day shift starts arriving. There is bustle, comings and goings among the staff. Elevators come into use again. It's still very early but not the dead of night any more. A good time to do the unexpected.

That was my strategy. Malory had never seen Sonia except helpless in bed. We had insisted all along on keeping her safe in her suite while tempting Lew to come there. There was a good chance that Malory hadn't covered the other possibility quite as thoroughly, a chance that his men were psychologically prepared to watch for an entrance and not an exit. Misdirection. It was bound to work.

And it did, as far as the cops were concerned. Sonia and I walked down one flight of stairs, got on the elevator and went all the way to the basement. Alex had gone on ahead carrying the packsack with the $200,000. Two are less noticeable than three. We were dressed in hotel uniform smocks organized previously by Chester. So we could walk out the employee exit quite openly. As if going off work or for a short break before the morning rush. And no one stopped us, no one asked us our business. Malory's men were clearly watching for a man trying to sneak in, not for women walking out.

Sonia and I got to the hotel parking lot and looked around for Alex. Something was badly wrong, she was nowhere to be seen. Hiding Sonia behind an enormous garbage container, I went to investigate. And I found Alex all right—semi-conscious between two parked cars, the packsack with the money gone.

"I'm OK, I'm OK," Alex panted. "Ambush. Just saw a movement then boom! I was out. Hell, and the money's gone." She was sitting up taking notice and seemed all right.

"Sit tight, I've got to get Sonia," I said. And ran knowing I would be too late. Sonia was not where I had left her. The timing had been perfect. I looked around. A familiar white Volvo was picking up speed only yards away. I sprinted towards it and in the process almost got run over by an old rusty, orange Datsun. As arranged, inside the Datsun were Betty and Lew. But Sonia, Sonia was in the white Volvo!

I wrenched open the Datsun door, jumped in and yelled,

"Get after that Volvo! Sonia's inside! Walter's got her!"

Betty accelerated immediately. The chase was on.

The white station wagon sped away from us along the wide, almost empty street. Betty Grelick concentrated on driving, using the old Datsun's gears like a CanAm driver. We couldn't count on speed to catch the newer, more powerful Volvo. But city streets aren't designed for speed. Knowledge of the city and fast reflexes gave us a chance.

"What's happening? What's going on?!" Lew Davies was alone in the back of the Datsun. That's where he had hoped to cozy up to Sonia and explain his dealings with Karl. I ignored him and talked calmly to Betty. To keep her steady and on her toes.

"Betty, if he's as smart as I think he is, he'll try to get on one of the expressways where his speed will be more of an advantage. You know Walter, answer me this: one—where is he trying to take Sonia? Do you know of any likely place?"

"No. I haven't any idea. He would know all sorts of places out of town where he goes to get his junk."

"OK. Two—how well does he know the city? By car that is. He doesn't own a car, does he?"

"To my knowledge he doesn't, he has the keys to Sonia's Volvo. Rents a truck for his junk hunting. I would say he doesn't know the city all that well."

"Good. So he's likely to stick to main streets. How about

you? D'you know the alleys in midtown Toronto? Hey, he's still going north. That's odd."

Betty nodded and grinned.

"Right, right. I know this town. Alleys are my specialty. He's going north, likely to cut over to the Parkway. That's a route he would know for getting out of town. Perhaps via St. Clair to Bayview. I'll try to head him off."

We roared through a red light. Davies sat very still behind us holding on to the back of the seat.

"He could be planning to double back as soon as we disappear from his rear view mirror," I went on to Betty.

The big white car ahead of us turned on Bloor Street and sped towards the Bloor Street viaduct to the Danforth. The early morning traffic was sparse. Lauker was making good time. Then instead of continuing to the nearest Parkway entrance he made a sudden left turn and zipped into elegant Rosedale. Without a moment's hesitation Betty cut across approaching traffic and sneaked down to Mount Pleasant Road a block ahead of him. I could see her reasoning. If she was right we had a chance. If not, not.

"Now you're cooking!" I said, and started to struggle out of the uniform smock. Our pursuit was in good hands. A moment later we saw the Volvo entering Mount Pleasant behind us! He was boxed in, the road here is divided by a concrete fence, no U-turns are possible on this stretch. Betty straddled the white line and slowed down. He had no choice but to try for a quick right turn at first opportunity. That brought him into Rosedale's maze of posh winding streets.

We saw him make the turn; Betty immediately reversed and we plunged backwards.

"Hold on to your hat!" I hollered happily. We were back in close pursuit, leaving a few angry motorists cursing behind.

"The cops must be on to this chase by now," I said.

"I just hope this orange wonder can make it. It's about ready for the scrap heap," Betty said, eyes on the road, her hands spinning the car like a top. "Belongs to one of the guys in the Herd. It's all we could beg, borrow or steal."

"He's headed for the Bayview Extension," I said.

"Right."

And so he did. Once on it our chances dimmed. He hit the Parkway at 140 kilometers per hour. Our Datsun groaned and shook, well past its limits. We would never keep up. Walter would get away, with Sonia.

Suddenly the Volvo swerved left, then right as if out of control. Close behind it, Betty pumped her brakes, holding to the steering wheel for dear life. I reached over and hit the horn button. Both cars left the road, careening over the grass verge. As we got nearer I saw that Sonia was fighting with Lauker and the wheel.

"We got him," I said and prepared to leap out. As I did, I heard the scream of police sirens approaching from all sides. I didn't wait. The Volvo crashed against a barrier. I saw Sonia drop. The driver's door sprung open discharging Lauker almost at my feet. The fight was short and vicious. I laced into him like a madwoman. Fighting wasn't his forte. By the time Betty and Lew got to us I had an arm lock on him.

"Go see about Sonia," I gasped. "I've got him."

The first cops arrived and relieved me of Walter Lauker. I told them to call Malory right away and went over to the white car. Sonia was still in the car, huddled on the seat. There were new bruises on her face, torn bandages made her look like a wounded warrior. Betty was looking after her. I looked in the back. The packsack lay on the seat. It was half empty. Half the money was gone. One hundred thousand dollars!

Of course it didn't matter right then. Sonia was safe, that's what mattered. Lauker in custody, that's what mattered. But the missing money did help to answer a question that had been nagging at me ever since I had found Alex lying there in the hotel parking lot. How had Lauker known we would be sneaking out the back door? And about the packsack, about Sonia, Alex and me in our uniform smocks? There was only one answer. Chester. My old pal and colleague, Chester. For $100,000 he would've sold his mother. As it was he'd only sold Sonia to Walter Lauker.

The world is full of decent people, but very few of them are in the detective business.

30

THERE ISN'T MUCH MORE TO TELL. My immediate problem, after we started to sort it all out was to pacify Malory. It wasn't easy for him to accept that I'd had to play it this way. He wasn't happy with me. I was sort of sorry about that but it couldn't be helped. Having cops mad at me is another occupational hazard.

Malory was soon too busy with the case against Lauker, collaring Chester and attending to a thousand and one details of police business to bother with me. We parted on reasonably good terms.

And Sonia? She had to go back to bed, under doctor's care. But she was well, better than ever. I sat with her a few days later. We talked over the case. I explained that Lauker intended to be a rich widower. How he resented her leaving him, resented her career, her million dollars, the $500 handout.

"So you were right about that. Boy, have I ever been blind! How about Betty?"

I explained about Betty. Betty and Lew. She had been Davies' partner in a coke delivery system. Small time but—enough. Sufficient to make her cooperative. Up to a point.

Sonia understood. She chuckled. Then said softly, "She did good, didn't she? Driving, I mean."

"She did very good. And so did you. We couldn't have caught up with that Volvo if you hadn't wrestled Lauker and got the car off the road. It was damn brave of you."

"We all did good." Sonia smiled at me. Then she dismissed our common exploits and concentrated on questions.

"That awful explosion. That bomb in your truck. That wasn't Walt, was it? It was Karl, right?"

"Yes, that was Karl's work. Trying to get rid of me. Walter egged him on. I suspect they had a hate session in the Tri-Met parking lot just after that performance after lunch. Karl did his favourite phone trick and had the security guard called away. Then—bingo!"

"Boy, what a mess. Listen, Helen, as soon as I'm out of here, I want to get away. Take a trip. Will you be getting a new truck with your insurance? Also remember, you'll have a fat fee from me."

I tried not to jump to any conclusions about what she might be leading up to.

"Yes, I'm in the market for another truck or van. I think I'll check out other makes. Then I'm on my way west, at last. To the coast. Home."

I held my breath.

"Can I come along with you? I've never done a trip like that. A truck and a tent and all the time in the world! I won't be a bother, I promise. Please!"

Now I had to believe it. Sonia wanted to come west with me! Dreams do come true.

"Sure," I said. "That would be great."

And it was. But that's another story.

▼